"We have a duty to Jemima, a responsibility."

Liv paced back into the living room to stare down at the sleeping baby. She was an innocent in all of this.

Liv had known Jemima for all of three days, and yet she'd do anything now to protect her.

She rose and spun around to find Sebastian right behind her. She took an instinctive step backward, the scent of cinnamon and something darker like aniseed wrapping about her. With a smothered oath he seized her shoulders before she could fall over the baby carrier.

"Careful." He moved her three steps away from it.

The warmth of his hands burned through the thin material of her jumper, sending a drugging surge of heat coursing through her blood.

His hands dropped abruptly back to his sides, and this time it was he who took a hasty step back. "Sorry, I didn't mean to startle you."

"No problem," she said before gesturing that they should return to the kitchen.

She preceded him. When she turned back, she found him staring down at the baby with such gentleness her heart turned in her chest. He reached down to pull the cover up around the baby more fully. "Don't you worry about a thing, little one. I'll find your mama for you. I promise."

"Yes," she said, before she even realized she was going to say anything.

He turned to stare at her, straightened. "Yes?"

"To your solution. I think it's a good one. Just let me pack a bag."

Dear Reader,

Ever since I was a little girl I've been fascinated by twins. I so wanted to be a twin. I whiled away many an idle hour dreaming I'd been adopted, separated from my twin at birth, fantasizing how one day we'd be reunited. Mind you, I didn't want to be just any twin—I wanted to be an *identical* twin. Just the thought of being able to switch places without anyone knowing filled me with glee.

In hindsight, it's probably just as well I don't have an identical twin. I suspect too much trouble would've ensued. :) But one of the best things about being a writer is the opportunity to vicariously play out one's fantasies in the pages of a book. Hence, *A Baby in His In-Tray*, my twin-swap story, was born.

Add into the mix an abandoned baby, a grumpy boss and an historic mansion right out of the pages of a Jane Austen novel and you have the recipe for a whole lot of fun and games...along with a large serving of nail-biting agitation when attraction and love raise the stakes.

I hope you enjoy Olivia and Sebastian's journey to a happily-ever-after as much I did.

Hugs,

Michelle

A Baby in His In-Tray

—

Michelle Douglas

ISBN-13: 978-1-335-13505-6

A Baby in His In-Tray

First North American publication 2018

Copyright © 2018 by Michelle Douglas

All rights reserved. Except for use in any review, the reproduction or utilization of this work in whole or in part in any form by any electronic, mechanical or other means, now known or hereafter invented, including xerography, photocopying and recording, or in any information storage or retrieval system, is forbidden without the written permission of the publisher, Harlequin Enterprises Limited, 22 Adelaide St. West, 40th Floor, Toronto, ON M5H 4E3, Canada.

This book is a work of fiction. Names, characters, places and incidents are either the product of the author's imagination or are used fictitiously, and any resemblance to actual persons, living or dead, businesses, companies, events or locales is entirely coincidental.

This edition published by arrangement with Harlequin Books S.A.

For questions and comments about the quality of this book, please contact us at CustomerService@Harlequin.com.

® and TM are trademarks of the publisher. Trademarks indicated with ® are registered in the United States Patent and Trademark Office, the Canadian Intellectual Property Office and in other countries.

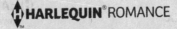

HARLEQUIN®ROMANCE

ISBN-13: 978-1-335-13505-6

A Baby in His In-Tray

First North American publication 2018

Printed in U.S.A.

www.Harlequin.com

Michelle Douglas has been writing for Harlequin since 2007, and believes she has the best job in the world. She lives in a leafy suburb of Newcastle, on Australia's east coast, with her own romantic hero, a house full of dust and books and an eclectic collection of '60s and '70s vinyl. She loves to hear from readers and can be contacted via her website, michelle-douglas.com.

Books by Michelle Douglas

Harlequin Romance

The Vineyards of Calanetti

Reunited by a Baby Secret

The Wild Ones

Her Irresistible Protector
The Rebel and the Heiress

The Redemption of Rico D'Angelo
Road Trip with the Eligible Bachelor
Snowbound Surprise for the Billionaire
The Millionaire and the Maid
A Deal to Mend Their Marriage
An Unlikely Bride for the Billionaire
The Spanish Tycoon's Takeover
Sarah and the Secret Sheikh

Visit the Author Profile page
at Harlequin.com for more titles.

For Beth,
whose quirky and offbeat sense of humor
always makes me laugh.

Praise for
Michelle Douglas

"Captivatingly sweet! Great characters, a
heartwarming story line and just a whole lot of
feel-good reading!"

—*Goodreads* on *The Spanish Tycoon's Takeover*

CHAPTER ONE

'WHAT I'M SAYING, Liz, is that someone has left a baby on your—*my*—' she amended, aware that Liz had already corrected her twice so far this phone call '—desk!'

'A baby?' Liz parroted for the third time, and Olivia Grace Gilmour closed her eyes and dragged in a breath—a long, deep, calming breath. In through her nose and out through her mouth. No matter how much she might want to, she couldn't take her twin to task for her incredulity. She could hardly believe it herself.

Except seeing was believing.

She peered once more into the baby carrier at the sleeping infant.

'Livvy, I…'

Liv waited but nothing else was forthcoming, and her heart rate kicked up another notch.

'Where's Judith?'

Judith was Liz's assistant. 'She called in sick.'

'Good.'

'Good?' She tried to keep the shrill note out of her voice. A partner in confusion and concern would be welcome at the moment. But Liz was right. It was just as well Judith wasn't here to witness her panic. Liv didn't want to give the game away. She swallowed and tried to modulate her voice. 'There was a letter addressed to your boss tucked into the side of the baby carrier.'

'*Your* boss,' Liz corrected. If a voice could sound green, hers sounded green.

'*My* boss,' Liv managed through gritted teeth.

Never had agreeing to stand in for her twin at her day job seemed a crazier move than it did right at this very moment. But it was only for a week and Sebastian Tyrell—Liz's boss—was away. Not that he sallied forth all that often from his estate in Lincolnshire, from where he apparently oversaw operations. But with him being away it meant she shouldn't even need to speak to him on the phone. This week should've been non-eventful, mission possible, a walk in the park. Liz had promised her it'd be a piece of cake.

Except now there was a baby.

Somewhere in the back of her mind maniacal laughter sounded.

She stared into the carrier at the cherubically sleeping baby—the teensy-tiny baby. 'Heavens, Liz, it's little. She can't be more than four or five months old.'

'Oh, God.' If possible, Liz's voice turned greener. Liv grimaced. Her twin had never been good with babies. And now—

'Have you read the letter?'

Liv swung away from the baby, seized the letter and paced to the window overlooking a busy inner-London street, a sliver of the Thames in the distance, glinting silver in the afternoon light.

'Of course I've read the letter!' It was why she'd rung. It gave no clue whatsoever to the baby's identity. And she had no idea what to do. 'It says *"Sebastian"*—not *Dear*, not *Seb*, but *"Sebastian—I can't do this any more. It's not fair. You owe me. Do not let baby Jemima down!"*' She glared at the inoffensive-looking piece of paper. '*"Not"* is underlined three times. It ends in an exclamation mark.' She pulled in another long breath. 'It's not signed.'

'Not signed?' Liz's voice rose. 'Dear God, Livvy, I'm stuck in Turkey in the middle of a plane strike. It'll take me days to get home and—'

'Relax, Liz!' The words shot out of her with more confidence than she'd dreamed possible, but she recognised the panic in her twin's voice and needed to allay it. Liz was pregnant and she needed to stay calm. 'I'm not asking you to come home. You need to stick to your plan.'

What Liz didn't need was additional stress. Dear God, her sister had enough on her plate at the moment. Liv mentally kicked herself for troubling Liz with this except…except she'd panicked herself. 'Look, seriously, I can take care of everything at this end. I was just keeping you apprised of developments like I promised I would.' She dragged

a hand back through her hair. 'And I thought you might have some idea where this baby had come from.'

'I haven't the foggiest. I can't think of a single baby he has in his life.'

'Well...obviously somewhere along the line he became a father.'

A strangled noise on the other end of the phone was Liz's only reply.

She swallowed. Did Liz's boss even know he had a child?

'Oh, what a mess! But Livvy, I can't shed any light on this at all. I wasn't joking when I said the most personal thing Mr Tyrell and I have ever shared was our mutual concern over an accountant I'd hired. I mean, I hardly ever see him, the only thing we ever discuss is work...and that as briefly as possible as a rule. He's not a chatty man.'

'Seriously? Nothing personal? Ever?' She still couldn't get her head around that.

Liz was silent for a moment. 'When I returned from my holiday he asked me if I had a nice time. I said yes. That was the extent of the discussion.'

The holiday where Liz had become pregnant to her hot mystery man?

'No passing comments about politics and the state of the nation, or a book you've been reading, or a movie you've seen?' she persisted.

'*No!* We have a weekly phone call—the Tyrell Foundation is his baby and it's obviously close to his heart—but that's it. He's busy doing whatever it is lords running their estates are busy doing. It's the reason I was so convinced we could pull this switch off.'

They'd thought it so unlikely that Liv would even need to speak to him that they'd practically considered it a *fait accompli*. But now… She swallowed and nodded. She could do it. She could pull it off. After all, she'd had no trouble convincing Judith that she was Liz.

Still…deceiving the sixty-two-year-old Judith who did a solid job at maintaining the foundation's database but who was more interested in sneaking in a surreptitious game of Solitaire than gossiping with Liv was one thing. Deceiving a businessman in his prime was a different matter altogether.

'Livvy?'

'This new development might mean me and your Mr Tyrell have to come face to face.'

'Will you be OK with that?'

She could practically see the grimace on her twin's face. 'Yes.' She gave a silent scream and then stuck out her chin. 'But I'm not changing my hair.'

Finally Liz laughed. 'We already agreed I'd have to lop a few inches off mine before I came home. And in the unlikely event he even sees it,

let alone mentions it, I'll tell him I've gone back to being blonde.'

For a moment she could almost picture her twin waving an unconcerned hand through the air, treating the issue of hair as a matter of little importance. Liv couldn't help smiling. She loved her hair. 'Right. We'll call that Plan A, then.'

'What are you going to do now, though? About the baby?'

She suspected what she should do was call the police, but…

'Please don't lose me my job, Livvy.'

But there was that—it was what she was here for. Everything else in Liz's life was up in the air and she was clinging to the security of her job like a lifeline. Liv couldn't jeopardise that.

And if Mr Tyrell did happen to be the father of this baby…well, it wouldn't be fair to call the authorities until after she'd spoken with him.

'I'm going to ring your—*my*—boss and ask *him* what *he* wants to do about the situation. I'll do my best to sound cool and efficient—' like her twin '—but if I sound a tiny bit flustered I think, given the circumstances, that'll be understandable.'

'Oh, Liv, are you sure you don't want me to come home? I can do my best to get back asap. Given this rotten plane strike, if Mr Tyrell is out of the country it could take him days to get home too. And in the meantime you could be literally left holding the baby on your own.'

'Which sounds like more fun than doing government grant acquittals. There's not been a peep from the little tyke. And before you ask—yes, she's breathing. I checked. Besides, I love babies—you know that. And thankfully they're not actually all that much trouble at this age.

'Except for the four-hourly feeds and the sleep deprivation.' Liv glanced down at the baby and grinned. 'Not much sleep deprivation happening here. Besides, Mr Tyrell is bound to know who Baby Jemima is and what I should do with her. We'll sort it out.'

'I'm so, *so* sorry, Liv. If I'd thought for a moment that anything like this would happen, I'd have never asked you to fill in for me.'

'I know. But don't fear—I'll muddle on through. You just focus on sorting things out at your end. Don't worry about me, I'll be fine.'

Liv hung up from her twin and tucked her phone back into her handbag. She stared again at the sleeping baby and bit her lip. It *was* usual for babies to sleep a lot, right? She touched her fingers to the baby's forehead, but the baby didn't feel hot or feverish.

What on earth was the poor little mite going to think when she woke up and found her mother gone? 'Poor little chick.'

Right.

She planted herself in her office chair and pulled the phone towards her, punching in the contact number that Sebastian Tyrell had left...along with the instruction *Only to be used in the direst of emergencies.*

The phone rang three times before it was answered. 'Ms Gilmour.'

'Yes.'

'I trust this is an emergency?'

The cold, clipped tones told her it had better be or there'd be hell to pay. She took an immediate dislike to the man. 'Yes, I'm afraid it is.'

'My parents...?'

His tone didn't change and she disliked him even more. 'To the best of my knowledge they're in excellent health. This has nothing to do with your parents. It's to do with—'

Baby Jemima chose that moment to let loose with a loud wail.

Heavens! Who knew something so small could produce a sound so fierce? She stood up to peer into the carrier—still perched on her desk where it'd been left—but the sight of Liv seemed to startle the baby further. Baby Jemima's face turned red as she started crying in earnest.

Oh, heck!

Sebastian Tyrell's voice boomed down the line at her. 'Is there a baby in my office?'

Technically, it was her office.

Actually, it was Liz's office.

'Hey, there, little one, hush.' She ran her hand across the baby blanket—over the baby's tummy—in an effort to impart some comfort. 'Shh, it's OK.' She spied the dummy pinned to the blanket and popped it into the baby's mouth. Baby Jemima immediately stopped crying and sucked on it greedily. Oh! She must be hungry.

'What is a baby doing in my office?'

She hated that voice—the cutting ice of it. 'That, Se—sir...' She quickly caught herself. Liz had told her that first names weren't used in the office. *Ever.*

She closed her eyes and pulled in a breath. She had to keep her wits about her. Slip-ups were not allowed. She couldn't let Liz down. It was Sebastian Tyrell's reserve, his distance—both physical and emotional—that had made them believe they could pull this deception off. They could still pull it off. She and Liz were identical twins—at least on the outside. He'd never be able to tell them apart. She *could* do this.

'Continue, Ms Gilmour. Stopping partway through a sentence is not only unprofessional, but irritating.'

Her chin shot up and her nostrils flared. 'I was hoping you could shed light on this particular emergency, *sir.* You see, the baby *is* the emergency.

It was left on my desk during my lunch hour…
along with a letter for you.'

'*What?*'

She held the phone a little further away from her
ear and refrained from pointing out that deafening
one's office manager wasn't particularly professional either. Or that having her eardrums blasted
was seriously irritating.

'You'll have to excuse me for having read your
letter, but I deemed the situation warranted it.' She
feared, though, that her tone told him she didn't
give a flying fig what he thought about her having read his letter.

Air hissed down the line at her. 'Read it out
loud.'

She did. Word for word. As few as they were.

Without being asked, she read the letter again,
allowing him time to process it. She waited for
him to respond. When he continued to remain silent she asked, 'What would you like me to do?'

'I'm thinking.'

She wanted to tell him to think faster. 'Do you
know baby Jemima?'

'No.'

'Do you know who her mother might be?'

'Ms Gilmour, I'd appreciate it if you'd stop pep-
pering me with questions.'

Jemima spat her pacifier out and set up a tooth-
ache-inducing wail. 'Mr Tyrell, there's a baby on

my desk that is evidently hungry and probably in need of changing—a baby that has obviously been abandoned by its mother. You'll have to excuse my impatience, I'm afraid.' She pulled in a breath. 'If you don't know who this baby is or who she belongs to, then the sensible thing to do would be to contact the police and hand her over to Social Services.'

'No!'

She blinked. So…maybe he did have a clue?

'This child's mother obviously thinks there's some connection between us, between the baby and me.'

'Or someone could be trying to take advantage of your aristocratic heritage,' she felt honour-bound to point out. Sebastian was Lord Tyrell's only son. The Tyrell family had that enormous estate in Lincolnshire. Not to mention a London house and a holiday villa somewhere on the Riviera.

She rubbed Jemima's tummy again, and tried to entice her to take her dummy—unsuccessfully. If anything the volume of her cries only increased.

'Going to the police has the potential to cause a scandal. The tabloids would have a field day.'

She rolled her eyes. What on earth was a scandal when a baby's welfare was at stake?

'And a scandal will affect the Tyrell Foundation. It's on a knife-edge already. I don't want to risk scaring away the benefactors I've been in negotiations with for the last few months. We've worked too hard for that.'

Sebastian's charity wasn't one of the glamorous ones featuring children or animals on their flyers. His charity assisted the recently unemployed in the over-fifties age bracket to find work.

From all that Liz had said, it was gruelling work too, and apparently Sebastian toiled like a Trojan. It wasn't something she'd have expected from an aristocrat's son.

We all have our peccadilloes, she reminded herself. She'd have never expected to be particularly fluent in office work, and yet here she was.

She tossed her head and gritted her teeth. She was glad she'd become skilled enough to help her sister out of a tight spot.

Baby Jemima's continual crying scratched through her brain, making her temples throb. 'Where on earth are you anyway?'

A heavy sigh came down the line. 'Australia.'

'Australia!' She said a rude word.

'Ms Gilmour, did you just swear?' There was no censure in his voice, just astonishment.

'I can't stand this crying another second. I need to change and feed the baby. I'll call you back.'

Without further ado, she hung up on him.

Don't lose me my job, Livvy.

She grimaced before pouncing on the bag the absent mother had evidently packed for the baby.

She'd searched it for clues earlier. It contained clothes, toys, nappies, formula and bottles, and, most importantly of all, a set of instructions. A quick glance at them told her that Jemima's next feed had been due fifteen minutes ago.

She crooned nonsense at the baby as she changed and then fed her. 'Don't you worry, little snuggly-wuggly Jemima. We'll have you fed and dry in no time. Would you like to hear a bit about me—my qualifications and what have you? Well, I'll have you know that I was *the* go-to babysitter when I was in high school. And believe me there were plenty of tots in Sevenoaks, Kent. And since then I've been made a godmother—twice! Once to baby Bobby and once to baby Matilda. So you see, I do have credentials. You're in safe hands.'

Jemima drank her bottle with an avid greed that made Liv laugh. 'You're simply lovely, little Jemima.'

The baby puked up on the sleeve of Liv's blouse when Liv burped her, and then promptly fell asleep again.

'Easy-peasy, nothing to it,' Liv murmured, gently placing her in the carrier again. 'If only I could curl up and go to sleep too. But no, not I. I now have to ring my sister's boss and apologise for hanging up on him. Grovel if I have to so he won't fire Liz. Wish me luck, little one.'

Without wasting any more time, she grabbed the phone and hit redial. It was picked up on the first ring. 'I'm sorry I hung up so abruptly, but I had to—'

'There's no need to apologise, Ms Gilmour. The noise was driving me to distraction as well and I'm not even in the same country, let alone the same room. It all sounds quiet now, though.'

'Baby Jemima has been changed and fed and, having thrown up on my blouse, is now blissfully asleep. All's well in Baby Land.'

'I'll replace your blouse.'

She blinked. 'That won't be necessary. It'll wash out.' She stared down at the sleeping baby and something inside her chest clenched. 'She really is the sweetest little thing. Would you like me to send you a photo?'

'Why?'

She shook herself. What was she thinking? Sebastian Tyrell didn't sound like the kind of man who oohed and aahed over cute baby pictures. 'Maybe...maybe she looks like her mother and that'll give you a clue to the baby's identity.'

'I...uh... OK.'

She was grasping at straws and they both knew it. Nevertheless she took a picture on her phone and sent it through to him.

A long silence ensued. 'Babies all look the same to me.'

She bit her lip. 'You don't have much experience with babies, do you?'

'No.'

She drummed her fingers against her desk. He'd ruled out the police, so… 'Do you want me to organise a nanny or some kind of babysitting service?'

'I may not know much about babies but I know business. Questions will be asked and the answers recorded. The baby's full details will need to be provided—a birth certificate may need to be produced.'

She doubted an actual birth certificate would be required, but she caught the gist of his concerns. They didn't know Jemima's full details. They barely knew any details at all! And if he was the baby's father…

Another long silence ensued—a silence that started to burn and chafe through her. 'Look, I don't know if you'll consider this any kind of solution, but Jemima can stay with me until you get back to London. How does that sound?'

'It sounds perfect.'

His relief was evident and it occurred to her now that those long silences of his had been strategic devices to lead her to the point of making this precise offer. She didn't know whether to be outraged or not.

'I understand this is a great imposition on you, Ms Gilmour, and you have my sincere gratitude.'

She chose not to be outraged.

'I also understand that you can't be expected to perform both nanny duties and office duties at the same time. Please organise a temp to take over in your absence. Judith performs her duties ably, but...' He trailed off. 'The woman you arranged to come in while you were on holiday was very good.'

'I'll check with the agency and see if she's available.' Playing nanny would be far more fun than playing office manager. And she couldn't help thinking that the further away from the office she was, the less the likelihood of her and Liz's deception being detected.

Win-win.

She glanced at the sleeping baby. Except what was baby Jemima winning? *Nothing.* She faced upheaval and an uncertain future. She bit back a sigh. Thankfully the baby was blissfully unaware of that fact.

'I hope your mother is all right,' she murmured.

'I beg your pardon?'

Oops! 'Oh... I was talking to the baby, but... Her mother must've felt in the direst of straits to leave her baby like this.'

And she'd left her baby in the care of Sebastian Tyrell. What did that show?

That she trusted him?

She swallowed. That he was the father?

'I'd prefer it, Ms Gilmour, if you refrained from enacting a Cheltenham tragedy.'

Her chin shot up. 'To be perfectly frank with you, *sir*, I'm not sure it much matters what you'd prefer. I'd have preferred not to have come back from lunch to find an anonymous baby abandoned on my desk. There's not only a mystery to solve—' who was the child's mother '—but a couple of serious issues to be dealt with too. I can't help feeling time is of the essence.'

Don't lose me my job, Livvy.

She grimaced and waited for him to take her to task for her insolence. He didn't. Instead there was that darn silence again. She suddenly laughed. 'You don't feel that you can reprimand me at the moment because you're in my debt.'

'I have no wish to reprimand you. You're worried, understandably so, and I share your concerns. I will own, however, to a little…surprise over your fieriness.'

She winced. She needed to tread carefully—channel her more level-headed sibling. 'Babies bring it out in me,' she offered weakly.

'I see.'

'I should go and let you make your travel arrangements.' She blinked. 'I mean…you are planning to return immediately, aren't you?' She'd simply taken that for granted.

'Absolutely.'

'Or perhaps you'd like me to organise your travel arrangements?' She gave a silent scream. Were they part of her job description? She had no idea.

'The arrangements are already underway.'

The tap-tapping noises in the background suddenly made sense. She wondered how many devices he had open in front of him besides his phone—his tablet *and* laptop perhaps? Those strategic silences suddenly took on a different complexion.

A moment later she dismissed that thought. No, she'd bet her life on the fact that Sebastian Tyrell was a master of the strategic pause.

'I'll be back in London as soon as I can.'

'Travel safe, sir.'

'Wait!'

She wanted away from him—now! Though she couldn't explain why. 'Yes?'

'I'd like you and the baby to move into my house on Regent's Park.'

Not a chance! 'I'm sorry, Mr Tyrell, but I'm not comfortable with that. I'll go back to my—' she gulped back the word *sister's*, covered it with a cough '—flat. I know where everything is there.'

'I—'

'Please don't waste time arguing with me.'

'Very well.'

She winced at the tightness of his voice.

'You're going to incur expenses—the baby will need things. Please charge them to my personal account. I insist that I take care of all the expenses.'

'OK, will do.' She made a mental note to keep all receipts.

'I hope to see you very soon, Ms Gilmour.'

And then he was gone. Liv scowled at the receiver, miffed beyond measure that she hadn't had the chance to hang up first. She dropped the receiver back into its cradle. 'I can hardly wait.'

Liv sat bolt upright in bed and grabbed her phone before it could ring again. The clock by the bed read five forty-four a.m. *Please don't have woken the baby!* She held her breath but no answering wail met her expectant ears. *Thank you, God!*

'What?' she growled into the phone without the slightest bit of grace. It was too early and she was too tired.

'Ms Gilmour?'

Oh, God! 'Mr Tyrell?'

A sigh heaved down the phone. 'For the last five minutes I've been knocking on your door. I understand that it's early, but I'm starting to worry that I'm disturbing your neighbours.'

'Don't you dare wake the baby!' she whisper-hissed at him. 'Don't make another sound on threat of…of something dire!'

She leapt out of bed and shot to the front door of Liz's flat, reefing it open as quietly as she could. Her finger halted halfway to her lips when she took in the man that stood on the other side. Six feet two inches of solid-muscled man stood there, bristling with square-jawed arrogance and wide-legged impatience. Dark chestnut hair, lighter on the ends, stood up at odd angles as if he'd repeatedly run his hand through it. She had to fight the impulse to reach out and smooth it down.

She swallowed. Liz had never mentioned how handsome Sebastian Tyrell was. *Why not?* A pulse started up in her throat, making her breath choppy and uneven. Sebastian Tyrell wasn't merely handsome—the man was hot with a capital H!

'I know I look a mess,' he growled. 'But you could have the manners to pretend to not notice. I've come directly from the airport, and it's taken me more than fifty hours to get here, so what do you expect? And, I might add, you don't look much better.'

Dear God, she was standing in the open doorway in her pyjamas. They were perfectly respectable. They covered everything adequately. Some would argue *more than adequately*.

He continued to stare at her. 'What have you done to your hair?'

She tried to smooth it down. It probably looked like a rat's nest, though she knew that wasn't what he referred to. 'A…a change is as good as a holiday,' she mumbled.

He looked as if he were going to say something more, but then blinked and shook himself. 'Are you going to let me in?'

'You *cannot* wake the baby.'

Sebastian took in the martial light in his office manager's eyes and raised both hands. 'Understood.'

He'd never seen Ms Gilmour so…undone, if that was the correct term. He could barely discern a trace of his cool, efficient office manager in the woman in front of him. Granted, he'd never knocked on her door at the crack of dawn and dragged her from her bed either.

And then there was her hair!

It took all his strength not to reach out and touch it, to track a strand's length to see if it contained some kind of magic.

He rolled his shoulders—jet lag.

To be fair, he'd never contemplated Ms Gilmour's life outside of the office before now either. To be brutally honest, he'd barely considered her at all beyond appreciating her myriad business skills and her efficiency…and feeling guilty about refusing her leave request a fortnight ago.

Damn it all to hell! She'd had no leave left. He'd needed her in the office overseeing things while he was overseas. He wasn't a tyrant, he was far from unreasonable, but he hadn't been able to shake off the memory of the desperation that had momentarily threaded through her voice. When the London office number had flashed up on his phone three days ago, he'd thought she'd rung to hand in her notice.

Had her hair been a response to her disappointment at having her leave declined?

He dragged both hands back through his hair. For heaven's sake, he'd not seen her in…what? Two months? She could've been wearing her hair like this the entire time.

He fought back a frown. He'd have sworn she wasn't the kind of woman who'd ever dye her hair like that. Evidently he'd misjudged her.

But then he had form for misjudging women.

He glanced at her again.

And tried to ease the knots in his shoulders. Her hair looked great—*really* great. He hoped it'd given her some solace.

He dragged his gaze from her hair to her face. She was staring at his chest as if hypnotised. 'Ms Gilmour?'

She didn't move.

'Ms Gilmour,' he repeated, a little louder.

She gave a violent start before pressing her finger to her lips. 'Shh.'

She looked as jet-lagged as he felt. A frown built

through him. 'How much sleep did you get last night?'

She held up two fingers.

He stiffened, but managed to keep his voice low. 'Two hours?' No wonder she looked so wrecked. For a crazy moment he had to fight an impulse to pull her into his arms and hug her, tell her to rest. He didn't, of course. It was a crazy notion. She'd probably slap him. And he'd deserve it. 'And the night before?'

Two fingers again.

He planted his hands on his hips. 'And the same the night before that?'

She nodded. 'Baby Jemima is a creature of the night. A demon. We—as in you and I—are not going to talk as we walk through the living room, because talking wakes her. We're not even going to look at her, because looking at her wakes her. You're going to follow me through to the kitchen and you're going to keep your eyes firmly forward the whole time. Got it?'

'Got it.'

Unfortunately eyes straight ahead meant his gaze was firmly fixed on her. Hips shouldn't move with such a provocative sway when encased in such ridiculously baggy garments. But apparently they could…and they did.

A pulse started up deep inside him and spread out until he throbbed with it. He wanted to dismiss it as jet lag, but he knew what it was—desire. And it had no place in his relationship with this woman. None whatsoever.

She gestured for him to take a seat at a small kitchen table, collapsing into the one opposite. 'I'm sorry,' she whispered, 'but I can't offer you coffee. The coffee machine is too loud. Apparently the kettle is too loud too, so I can't even offer you instant.'

He was dying for a coffee, aching for it. He now rued his decision to skip it at the airport to make his way here as quickly as he could instead. He wanted to sleep for a week, and yet he'd managed more sleep on the plane than she'd had in three days! 'I don't need coffee.'

'I do.' The words left her on a whimper. 'It's unfortunate on several counts. The primary one being that I don't function as a halfway decent person in the morning until after a shower and a mug of strong coffee.'

She dropped her head to her folded arms, every line of her etched in exhaustion. An answering exhaustion rose through him. He tried to smother a yawn. 'How much longer will the baby sleep for?'

She lifted her head to stare blearily at the clock on the wall. 'Probably another two hours…but it's one of those toss-a-coin things.'

Another yawn took him off guard. 'Maybe we should take advantage of that? Follow suit?'

She stared at him. 'Wow, you must be *really* tired.'

'Really tired,' he agreed. 'Spent.' But what he wanted was for her to jump back into bed and sleep until the lines around her eyes eased. 'Why don't you go back to bed and I'll stretch out on your sofa?'

'Reverse that and you have yourself a deal.' She shook her head when he went to argue. 'This is a one-bedroom flat. I can't offer you a spare bed, and I don't want to think what Jemima's reaction will be if the first thing she sees when she opens her eyes is a strange man.'

Ah. Right.

He insisted she take her duvet. He stretched out on top of her covers. He only meant to lie there for a minute—just to help straighten out the kinks in his spine—before checking his emails. While he caught up on his emails he could try and think of a practicable way forward where Jemima was concerned.

What on earth was he going to do with her? He closed his eyes and Ms Gilmour's autumn-hued hair filled his mind. A glorious fall of hair shaded in horizontal bands from a deep, dark auburn through to gorgeous oranges and finally a pale blonde. Shaded dark to light, from root to tip.

Gorgeous.

CHAPTER TWO

SEBASTIAN WOKE TO the scent of coffee. His nose told him it was seriously good coffee too. He sat up gingerly, stretched... All the kinks were gone. His back didn't hurt, his shoulders didn't hurt, his head didn't hurt.

He couldn't remember the last time he'd woken up feeling so rested!

Obviously a nap was exactly what he'd needed. A couple of hours to—

His jaw dropped when he caught sight of the bedside clock. It was after one-thirty *in the afternoon*. He'd been asleep for over seven hours?

Dear God! What would Ms Gilmour think? He'd left her holding the baby...*again*!

He shot out of the bedroom and came to a halt. His office manager turned from pouring out two steaming mugs of coffee to send him a smile that momentarily dazzled him. She looked utterly together. She looked like his efficient office manager again. Except rather than a black pencil skirt and business jacket she wore jeans and a jumper, and that magical autumn hair. And the smile.

'Come and have a coffee.'

He forced himself forward. He was careful not to look into the living room as he went past, even though he was sure the 'don't look at the baby' embargo had been lifted.

Critical eyes roamed over his face and she gave a satisfied nod. 'You look much better.'

He collapsed into a seat and pulled a mug of coffee closer. 'So do you. You managed to get more sleep?'

'A blissful three hours.'

She poured milk into her coffee. Whenever he visited the London office she drank it black—like him. But…she preferred it with milk? She did know she was free to order milk in for her coffee, didn't she? Where the Tyrell Foundation was concerned he'd accept the charge of penny pinching, but he could stretch to milk for his office manager's coffee.

'You should've woken me.'

'Why?'

'Because we have things to sort out.'

'People make better decisions when they're well-rested.'

She looked so perky and chipper he felt at a distinct disadvantage. He leaned across the table towards her. 'The baby?' he whispered.

'Happily engrossed with her baby gym at the moment,' she answered at a normal tone and volume. 'She's an absolute angel during the day. It's only at night she turns into a demonic creature from the deep.'

How could she sound so cheerful? She'd been sleep-deprived for three whole nights. How could she look so...delectable?

'Drink your coffee, and then have a shower while I make us some lunch and—'

'I couldn't possibly impose on you more than I already have—'

'You can and you will. You can't just up and leave with the baby. Besides, Jemima is due for a feed soon and then she'll go down for a nap. There's really not much point in trying to do anything before then. There's a fresh towel for you in the bathroom.'

He supposed she had a point. And he was dying for a shower.

He collected a few things from his suitcase— left by the front door when he'd arrived earlier. On his way past he peeked at the baby. She lay on a quilted rug, batting at the soft toys suspended above her. Her head wobbled around to look at him, the tiny body went rigid and then she let forth with such a piercing wail he had to cover his ears.

Ms Gilmour came racing in from the kitchen. 'What did you do to her?'

'Nothing! I... I just looked at her.'

'And what were you told?'

'Don't look at the baby,' he mumbled, feeling all of two inches tall.

She leant down to sweep the baby up in her

arms, cuddling the tiny body against her chest. Her jeans pulled tight around the soft swell of her backside and that damn pounding started up at the centre of him again, sending warm swirls of appreciation and need racing through his bloodstream.

He swallowed when she turned back around to face him.

'Did the big, bad man scare you, pretty girl? Did he sneak up on you and frighten you?'

He watched in amazement as baby Jemima snuggled into her rescuer, her crying ceasing as if a switch had been flicked. Ms Gilmour then blew a raspberry and the baby gave her a big smile and waved her arms about in evident delight.

'How…?' He stared at the baby and then his office manager. 'How did you do that? You took her from crying to laughing in seconds!'

She blew on her nails and polished them against her shoulder. 'Just call me Poppins, Mary Poppins.'

She said it in the same tones James Bond always used when introducing himself, *Bond, James Bond*, and he couldn't help but laugh.

She hitched the baby a little higher in her arms. 'Jemima, meet…' She frowned. 'What would you like her to call you?'

He had no idea. Did she have to call him anything? He frowned. Hold on, she couldn't call him anything. She was too young and——

One look at his extraordinary office manager told him that wouldn't wash. 'What does she call you?'

'Auntie…uh… Liz.'

Her gaze slid away, and he understood why. He knew her Christian name was Eliza, but he didn't want to call her that. He wanted things to remain on as formal a footing as possible.

He let out a long, slow breath. 'Uncle Sebastian,' he clipped out.

'Right. Baby Jemima, meet Uncle Sebastian.'

She said his name impersonally and yet something inside of him stretched and unwound as she uttered it.

He did his best to ignore it.

'Well, say hello,' she ordered him. 'Talk to her.'

He shuffled a step closer.

'Don't frown or you'll make her cry again.'

He smoothed out his face and tried to find a smile. 'Hello, Jemima, it's nice to meet you.' He fell silent. The baby frowned at him. 'What do I say?'

'Say something nice. Tell her she's pretty. Tell her you've been on a big plane…recite a poem. It doesn't matter. She just needs to know you're friendly.'

A poem? He used to love poetry. Once upon a time. It felt like a hundred years ago now. He pulled in a deep lungful of air. '"The Assyrian came down like a wolf on—"'

'Good God, not Byron!'

Both woman and child swayed away from him. 'You'll scar her for life.'

Behind those honey-brown eyes he had a feeling she was laughing at him.

'Can't you think of something more...cheerful?'

Cheerful? Inspiration struck. *'The Jabberwocky!'*

He recited the entire poem and both woman and child stared at him as if mesmerised.

'Give her your finger.'

He did as bidden. Jemima stared at it for a moment or two, swaying in her protector's arms, before reaching out and clasping it in one tiny fist. Something inside of him felt as if it were falling.

She pulled it closer and then up towards her mouth, but he gently detached himself from her grip. 'You might want to wait until I've washed my hands first. You've no idea where these have been.'

Jemima stared at him and then gave a big toothless grin before letting forth with a sound partway between 'Gah!' and a gurgle.

He could feel his entire body straighten—his chin came up and his shoulders went back—and he couldn't help smiling back. 'She smiled at me. She...she smiled.'

He glanced at his office manager to find her staring at him as if she'd never seen him before. Something arced in the air between them, and colour flooded her cheeks. She shook herself and sent him a smile that didn't hide the consternation in her eyes. 'You've just been given the official seal of approval.' She laughed and suddenly seemed more natural again. 'Hold tight to the memory. You might just need it at two o'clock in the morning, and at three…and four.'

It hit him then that she'd been right. He couldn't just walk out of here with Jemima. He was going to need help.

Her help?

Something inside him chafed at the idea. He had a feeling it'd be best for him and Ms Gilmour to get back on a professional footing asap. He could hire someone else. He'd have to come up with a cover story for Jemima of course, but…

'Mr Tyrell?'

But first he had to stop staring at her! 'I'll, uh, just go have that shower.'

When he emerged from the shower, he found Jemima asleep and his hostess making sandwiches.

'Egg and lettuce,' she said, setting two in front of him.

They ate in silence. She kept glancing across at him and he knew he should initiate the conversation, but he didn't know where to start.

'Do you have any idea who her mother might be?' she finally asked.

'None whatsoever.'

She pulled in a breath. 'I know we're straying into dangerously personal territory, but...can you recall all of the women you've been...intimate with in the last twelve to fifteen months?'

He choked on his sandwich. 'I'm not Jemima's father!'

One eyebrow kinked upwards. 'How do you know that for sure?' Her lips twisted. 'Contraception isn't always a hundred per cent effective.'

He knew that, but... Something in her tone caught at him. He frowned. 'You sound as if you're speaking from experience.'

Her gaze dropped to her plate. 'Second-hand experience. A, um...girlfriend.'

'I'm *not* Jemima's father.'

She glanced back up at him. 'How can you be so certain?'

Because he'd not slept with anyone in two years! But he had no intention of confessing that to this woman. It made him sound priestly, saintly, celibate, and he was none of those things.

'Have you kept in contact with them all?'

He grabbed the branch she'd unknowingly handed him. 'Yes.'

She leant back and folded her arms, staring at him in outright disbelief. It rankled.

'I don't know what kind of man you think I am, Ms Gilmour, but there haven't been an endless parade of women in and out of my bed. I know *every* woman I've slept with in the past two years, and I've kept in contact with *all* of them. I can assure you that none of them have become pregnant—not with me and not with anyone else.'

She unfolded her arms, but he didn't know if she believed him or not. He didn't know why it should matter so much to him either way. She was his office manager, not his moral guardian.

'Jemima and I can get DNA tests done if it'll put your mind at rest,' he snapped out. 'A paternity test.'

Luscious lips—lips he'd never realised were luscious until this moment—pursed. 'Could you, though? You've not been made Jemima's legal guardian. You don't have the authority to give legal consent for such a test.'

He opened his mouth. He closed it again. She had a point.

'Which is why,' she continued, 'I'm not going to let you leave here with Jemima.'

He blinked. Had she just said...? 'I beg your pardon?'

'I'm not letting you take the baby.'

He stared at her. 'You can't stop me.'

Their gazes locked and clashed. 'Do you mean to take Jemima by force?'

His hands clenched to fists. Of course he wasn't going to take the baby by force! Was she threatening him with the police? He pulled in a measured breath. 'Jemima's mother entrusted her to my care,' he reminded her.

'You'll have to excuse me for not putting much faith in Jemima's mother's reasoning.' She'd leapt up and now proceeded to pace—back and forth in agitated circles. 'She left Jemima in my office during my lunch break. What if I'd decided to take a half-day—to skive off because the boss was away?'

His head rocked back. 'You'd never do such a thing.'

'*I* know that and *you* know that, but she doesn't know me from Adam. So *she* couldn't know that.'

She had a point.

'She left the baby in your care but you were *out of the country*. What was she thinking? I mean, you *live* in Lincolnshire, not in London. Had she put any thought into this at all? Hadn't she done any research?'

He couldn't fault her reasoning.

She planted herself back in her chair. 'Look, this is all beside the point. I wish I wasn't involved. I don't want to be involved. But I am, and ethically and morally I can't just hand that baby over to you and walk away. Not when you aren't her father. Not when you know nothing about babies.'

He dragged both hands back through his hair. If their positions were reversed he knew he'd feel the same.

'Why do you want to take her anyway? Why do you feel so responsible for her?'

Finally they came to the crux of the matter. Exhaustion, disgust…and a still searing sense of betrayal momentarily overtook him. He dropped his head to his folded arms. Eventually he lifted it and met her gaze. 'I suspect Jemima and I are related.'

'Related?'

He forced himself to maintain eye contact. 'A niece perhaps.'

'But…you don't have any siblings.'

He had to swallow before he could speak. 'I have no siblings that I know about.'

'Ah.' She slumped back as if all the air had gone out of her.

'Or…' worse yet '…she could be my half-sister.'

'But—' she frowned and leaned towards him '—your father must be…'

'Sixty-eight—old enough to be her grandfather, yes.'

Liv ran a hand across her brow in an effort to shift the tightness that gripped it like a vice. The poor man looked exhausted. Not physically exhausted the way he had when she'd opened her door to him earlier, but deep-down-in-his-soul exhausted. 'I guess that explains the scandal you want to avoid.'

His head swung up to meet her gaze again. 'I've

given up trying to quash scandal where my parents are concerned.'

Given how often they appeared in the pages of the tabloids, that was probably just as well. It might also explain why Sebastian wanted to present such a squeaky-clean image himself.

She wanted to see him smile again, the way he had when Jemima had smiled at him. It was probably crazy, but... 'I don't believe half of what the papers say. They inflate everything.'

His lips twisted—not into a smile. 'Where Hector and Marjorie Tyrell are concerned, you can believe pretty much everything that you read.'

She winced.

'My parents are selfish people, Ms Gilmour, and have been all their lives. Chasing their own pleasure is more important to them than anyone's welfare.'

Including their son's? A weight pressed down on her chest.

'I've no interest in protecting their reputations—they don't have reputations worth protecting. However, if Hector has taken advantage of some young woman and left her feeling *desperate*, then she does deserve protecting. And until I can discover who she is, I mean to shield her from the spotlight.'

Liv lifted her chin. 'Good. Good for you!'

This time he did give a smile, though it was

only a small one…and tinged with disillusion. 'In the meantime we—' he gestured first to her and then to himself '—have this problem to sort out.'

'No problem,' she assured him. 'You go off and find Jemima's mother. In the meantime Jemima can stay here with me. Ms Brady is doing a fine job holding the fort at the office. I've been checking in with her every afternoon.'

'No.'

No? What did he mean, no?

'Just as you're not comfortable letting me take the baby, I'm not comfortable leaving the baby with you.'

She couldn't prevent air from hissing out between her teeth. 'You didn't seem to mind her spending the last three nights with me when it suited you. From memory, I had your *undying gratitude*.'

'I believe that's a slight embellishment.' Just for a moment light danced in his eyes, making him look younger and less troubled. 'But you mistake me, Ms Gilmour.'

The formality of that *Ms Gilmour* was starting to chafe at her, but she didn't have an answer for it. She didn't want him calling her Liz or Eliza. Every time he did it'd bring home, all the more acutely, the deception she was playing on him. She was finding it hard enough to maintain the charade as it was, without an additional load of guilt every time he called her by her sister's name. At least she *was* Ms Gilmour.

It's a situation of your own making.

Yes, thank you—she knew that well enough. She pulled in a breath. She only had to survive for another few days. 'I mistake you?'

'I don't doubt your ability to look after Jemima, and I don't doubt your integrity.'

Darn it all! Why did he have to make her sound mean-spirited for doubting him? 'Then why aren't you comfortable continuing our arrangement?'

'Because you're getting no sleep. It's not fair to ask you to continue in this vein. You live in a one-bedroom flat. You haven't a spare room to put the baby in, let alone any additional help I might be able to provide for you.'

She wished she hadn't been so utterly shattered when she'd opened the door to him earlier. She'd sounded—and acted—like a mad woman. It was all she could do not to wince. She'd hoped he'd been too jet-lagged to remember, but…apparently not. The impression she'd made on him had evidently been indelible.

'I have a solution if you're willing to hear it.'

He had the most perfectly shaped mouth. She'd love to paint it and—

Stop it! She didn't want to think about painting or Sebastian Tyrell's mouth or anything. She didn't want to like him!

She rose and went to check on the baby. She returned to her seat only when she had her wayward thoughts back under lock and key. 'OK, hit me with it.'

He raised an eyebrow.

Oops, that was probably a bit informal for Liz. 'I mean, please outline your solution, Mr Tyrell. I'm all ears.'

He stared at her with pursed lips. 'I never imagined you'd be like this…outside of the office, I mean.'

His words had a texture and they brushed across her skin with a faint promise she didn't dare examine. It took all her strength to stop from chafing her arms. What did he mean? Like what? *Human?* She didn't ask. She didn't want to know. 'I wouldn't have expected you to think about what I was like outside of the office.'

He frowned and opened his mouth.

'Which is exactly as it should be,' she added.

He snapped his mouth shut, but his frown deepened. 'I want you to know that I'm more than happy for you to order in milk for your tea and coffee at the office.'

Oh! Liz took hers black! And he'd noticed that she'd added milk to hers earlier. *She was an idiot!* She tried to shrug. 'I chop and change all the time.' She shrugged again, overdoing it but unable to stop herself. 'Sometimes I prefer milk, sometimes I don't.'

His gaze narrowed in on her face. 'Well, on the weeks you do prefer milk you're to order it in. Are we clear on that?'

'Crystal,' she assured him.

Dear lord, that was sweet of him, and she felt an utter cow. She and Liz were the ones deceiving him. He had *nothing* to feel guilty about.

You're not doing it to hurt him. Besides, you're helping him.

She *was* helping him. And, given the events of the last few weeks, it was just as well that she was here rather than Liz. She was much better able to cope with a baby. Liz may, in fact, have gone to pieces. But that knowledge didn't make her feel any the less guilty.

'Well…ahem…tell me about this solution of yours.'

He set both hands on the table and leaned towards her. The scent of something rather lovely like spiced apples drifted across to her. 'We all leave together and go to my house on Regent's Park.'

Move in with him? Ooh, she really didn't want to do that. Instinct told her that the more distance she kept between herself and Sebastian the better.

'There's ample room in the house and you can

still be Jemima's primary carer, but with the added benefit of having help near at hand.'

She bet he had an entire army of household staff. And a huge house. It was quite possible they'd hardly ever see each other.

'And…you'll do your best to find Jemima's mother?'

He nodded. 'That's the plan. I don't care what it takes, I *will* find her.'

Liv thought hard. She wasn't sure she could deal with too many more sleepless nights. If Jemima's mother had had to put up with that for months… With no help, no family… Liv repressed a shudder, understanding in a way she never had before how that kind of pressure could make a person snap.

But surely, after a little rest, Jemima's mother would come forward to claim her? And she'd find them quicker and easier if they were at Sebastian's house.

'If you think I'm being irresponsible in any way you can still carry out your original intent and go to the police.'

'Oh!' She shot to her feet. 'That wasn't a threat. It—'

'I know, and I understand. We have a duty to Jemima, a responsibility. You've been thrust into a role you didn't ask for, but you and the baby have bonded. And now you're understandably reluctant to abandon her to an uncertain fate. It's admirable.'

She paced back into the living room to stare down at the sleeping baby. She was an innocent in all of this. She knelt down beside her, brushed her fingers over a tiny hand.

The hand opened and gripped one of Liv's fingers convulsively before loosening again as she drifted back into a deep sleep. It was as if that little hand had squeezed Liv's heart. She'd known Jemima for all of three days, and yet she'd do anything now to protect her.

She rose and spun around to find Sebastian right behind her. She took an instinctive step backwards, the scent of cinnamon and something darker like aniseed wrapping about her. With a smothered oath he seized her shoulders before she could fall over the baby carrier.

'Careful.' He moved her three steps away from it.

'Sorry, I, um…didn't realise you were standing right there.' *So close!* 'You startled me.'

The warmth of his hands burned through the thin material of her jumper, sending a drugging surge of heat coursing through her blood. He stared down at her and his pupils dilated. This close to him she could see the lighter flecks—almost silver—in the grey of his eyes.

His hands dropped abruptly back to his sides and this time it was he who took a hasty step back. 'Sorry, I didn't mean to startle you.'

She swiped suddenly damp palms across the seat of her jeans. 'No problem,' she said, before gesturing that they should return to the kitchen.

She preceded him. When she turned back, she found him staring down at the baby with such gentleness her heart turned in her chest. He reached down to pull the cover up around the baby more fully. 'Don't you worry about a thing, little one. I'll find your mamma for you. I promise.'

'Yes,' she said before she even realised she was going to say anything.

He turned to stare at her, straightened. 'Yes?'

'To your solution. I think it's a good one. Just let me pack a bag.'

It took nearly half an hour in a black cab to drive from Liz's southside suburb to Sebastian's home—just off the outer circle of Regent's Park. The cab stopped in front of a neo-classical terrace—all white brick and imposing columns. 'You...you live here?' she breathed.

Sebastian didn't answer. He was already out of the cab, busy paying the driver and collecting up the various bags. She went to help him, but he shook his head. 'You just take care of Jemima.' He handed her a key and then hitched his head in the direction of the...*mansion*. 'Let yourself in.'

She stared at the black front door. Just...wow! Did he own the entire building or had it been converted into apartments? She glanced down at the key. She guessed there was only one way to find out.

She unlocked the door to find a large entrance hall complete with a fancy chandelier. A grand staircase curved gracefully to the upper floors. Reception rooms ranged off on either side. So... not a converted flat, then.

She moved the baby carrier to the other hand. 'Hello?'

'Who are you calling for?'

Sebastian came bustling in behind her. He set her bag, two of Jemima's bags and the portable cot that Jemima refused to sleep in down on the floor. His suitcase and several other bags still stood on the footpath.

'I... Your staff. I didn't want the appearance of a strange woman with a baby to make anyone nervous.'

'I don't have staff.'

He turned and headed back outside to collect the rest of their bags.

She could feel her eyes start from their sockets. What did he mean, he didn't have staff?

'Mrs Wilson comes in three days a week to clean,' he said, when he came back in. 'But I have no live-in staff.' He set the remaining bags down. 'I'm rarely in London.' He shrugged. 'It'd be indulgent, unnecessarily extravagant.'

And she was quickly coming to realise that he was neither of those things. Unfortunately that only made her like him all the more.

'You seem surprised.'

She moistened suddenly dry lips. 'So when you said I'd have help with the baby...?'

His face cleared. 'I meant me—that I'd help you. We can take it in shifts.'

A vision of spending the late hours of the night with him rose up through her mind with disconcerting clarity. Ooh, no...that couldn't happen and—

'That is OK, isn't it?'

But in the next instant she remembered the Jekyll and Hyde act Jemima pulled as soon as the sun went down and the image dissolved. There'd be no opportunity for any...funny business. Which was just as well, she told herself in her sternest voice.

'Ms Gilmour?'

She shook herself. 'Yes, of course that's OK. I just feel a bit of an idiot now for expecting staff.'

He hefted bags into his hands. 'My parents would tell you I'm the idiot.'

'They'd fill the place with an army of staff, I take it?'

'They would.'

She grabbed the nappy bag and followed him towards the staircase. 'You know what? I don't think I'd like your parents very much.'

'You'd be one of the few. They're widely considered...eccentric but charming'

She wrinkled her nose. 'Well, the likelihood of me meeting your parents, Seb—'

She froze at her slip.

He stilled.

Everything inside of her crunched up tight. 'Oh, God, I'm sorry. That was awfully unprofessional of me. Blame sleep deprivation. I promise it won't happen again, *Mr Tyrell*.'

He set his bags on the floor. He took the nappy bag and baby carrier from her and put both down—gently—as well. He turned her to face him, before planting his hands on his hips. Her mouth dried as she took in the long line of his legs—their latent power barely disguised by his business trousers—those lean hips tapering up to intriguingly broad shoulders.

'I think this is an issue we ought to clear up right now.'

'You'd be one of the first. I've never wished I wasn—'

She wrinkled her nose. 'Well, the likelihood of me meeting your parents just—'

CHAPTER THREE

'WE NEED TO sort this out,' Sebastian repeated.

'Sort what?' she squeaked.

She stared at him with wide eyes as if afraid he was going to give her a right royal rollicking. Damn it all to hell! What kind of grump was he to have her looking at him like that?

'I didn't say you were a grump!'

It was only then he realised he'd said the words out loud. 'You're staring at me as if you think I'm going to haul you across the coals.'

'Sorry, I—'

She broke off to press the heels of her hands to her eyes. He dragged a hand back through his hair and fought the urge to draw her into the circle of his arms and press her head to his shoulder where she could rest. She must be dead-on-her-feet tired. He'd got a good, solid seven hours' sleep, but not her. 'I'm *not* upset that you started to call me by my first name.'

She pulled her hands away, her eyes wary. 'You're not?'

'No.' He'd liked the sound of his name on her lips.

She pressed her hands tightly together in front of her and stared down at them. 'Nevertheless,

I think it's important to maintain professional boundaries.'

His chest clenched tight. When had he become so self-absorbed? For the last two years he'd sought refuge in an impersonal distance in both his professional and personal life. He thought his coolness had created a corresponding coolness in all those around him, but it was obvious that, like him, Ms Gilmour sought detachment.

And he had no right to intrude further into her life than he already had, to ask anything more of her beyond the employer-employee relationship. Except…

Baby Jemima demanded more from both of them and it appeared they were both more than willing to unstintingly give the baby whatever she needed.

He just had to make sure that whatever price was paid, it wasn't too high for the woman standing in front of him.

'Several years ago I made the very grave mistake of mixing business with pleasure.' She stared at her hands as if they held the key to the universe. 'I don't mean to ever make that same mistake again.'

He pondered her words. From memory she was twenty-five. Several years ago she'd have been very young. She'd called it a *grave mistake*. His hands clenched into fists. Someone had taken advantage of her innocence and had hurt her badly. If he ever got hold of the man who'd done that he'd—

'Look, I'm not saying that's what I think is going to happen in our situation.'

She stared at his fists, her eyes going wide and worried. He unclenched his hands immediately. 'Of course not. I never thought for a moment that's what you were suggesting. I was just thinking of what I'd like to do to the man who hurt you.'

'Oh.'

She shot him a smile—so sweet and lovely, it melted through him like treacle melting into the honeycomb of a hot crumpet, softening all of the stony places inside of him.

It took all of his concentration to keep his breathing even. He had to be careful around this woman. Once you opened yourself up to a baby, other walls were in danger of coming down. He had to keep them standing firm—for all their sakes. He was better than his parents, and he had no intention of blurring the line between business and pleasure himself.

'I think we can both agree,' he started carefully, 'that this current *surprising* situation that we find ourselves in is not exactly a professional one.'

'No, not precisely professional,' she agreed.

Her eyes remained trained on him, waiting.

'But this,' he gestured to the baby, 'is only a temporary interruption from our usual professional routine. When we get Jemima's situation resolved things will go back to how they were.'

She pursed her lips and then pointed to herself. 'Ms Gilmour.' And then pointed to him. 'Mr Tyrell.'

'Exactly.'

'But in the meantime you're suggesting…?'

'That perhaps, while we're not in the office, we can unbend enough to call each other by our first names.'

Her nose wrinkled.

Someone had really done a number on her, hadn't they?

But as he continued to survey her, it occurred to him that it wasn't him she didn't trust, it was herself. Something primal tried to claw its way to the fore—something that wanted to force the issue, force her to see him as a man rather than her boss, force her to take a risk.

He stiffened and beat it back down. He and his office manager were *not* going to dance that particular dance, regardless of how attractive or surprisingly intriguing he found her.

He was not opening himself up to betrayal again. *Ever.*

He'd keep his focus professional and his libido under wraps. He'd learned an important lesson with Rhoda, and it was one he had no intention of ever forgetting. He fought a sudden exhaustion.

He didn't have the heart—the energy—to venture down that path again. The part of him that had once welcomed the idea of love and family had been destroyed.

His office manager might be the complete opposite to Rhoda. But if she wasn't she'd be no good for him. If she were, he'd be no good for her. Either way someone would get hurt. He shook his head. *Not going to happen.*

Her need for distance and reserve should comfort him, but the thought of calling her Ms Gilmour in these circumstances rankled. 'You're not my office manager in this situation, you're...'

He watched the bob of her throat as she swallowed. 'I'm...?'

'Jemima's advocate, her friend...her Auntie Liz.'

She frowned and crossed her arms. 'You are *not* calling me Auntie Liz.'

She looked so suddenly schoolmarmish he had to choke back a laugh. 'How about I just call you Eliza?'

She huffed out a long breath, her lips pursed. She glanced away, finally giving a shrug before meeting his gaze once again, her expression strangely resigned. 'Fine. And I'll call you Seb.'

No one had ever shortened his name—not even at school. He liked it. At least...he liked it coming from her lips.

His collar tightened about his throat and he

had to resist the urge to run his finger beneath it. He couldn't let this become too cosy. First names didn't mean they had to become too familiar with each other. It wouldn't do. He and Eliza were not going to cross any other boundaries.

She pointed a finger at him. 'But this is only temporary. When we're back in our respective offices we're reverting to Mr Tyrell and Ms Gilmour...and all of this will feel as if it happened to somebody else.'

'Absolutely.' This was only a momentary loosening of clearly defined roles that would be assumed again as soon as this adventure was over. But would it be as easy to slip back into their old roles of Ms Gilmour and Mr Tyrell—boss and secretary—as they hoped it would be?

He shoved his shoulders back. He had to make sure it was. End of story.

'You did this for three nights *on your own*?' Sebastian looked at his office manager with a newfound respect. Before tonight he hadn't known that a baby's crying could grind you down to your soul so quickly. He hadn't known that once it started it refused to release you.

He hadn't known it could be so *relentless*!

'Don't look at me as if I'm some kind of hero.' She didn't even look up from rocking the baby. 'It was a case of needs must and nothing more.'

From ten o'clock last night through to now—almost two-thirty in the morning—Jemima had slept in odd twenty-to thirty-minute increments, only to wake again screaming. It seemed he couldn't do any damn thing right, at least not according to Jemima. He'd bounced, dandled, crooned, rocked, played teddy bears and choo-choo trains. He'd changed her and tried giving her a bottle—none of it had worked. She'd continue to cry through all his efforts, making him feel like a low-down loser. The only thing that made her stop crying was being in her new acting nanny's arms.

'I can't believe you didn't give me a harder time when I rocked up on your doorstep yesterday.'

She turned that amber gaze on him and raised an eyebrow. 'I thought I did give you a hard time.'

That made him laugh. She was a rank amateur compared to his parents. Compared to Rhoda.

All mirth fled at that thought.

'I can't believe you didn't shove her at me and push us both out of the door.'

'Do you hear what the big, bad man is saying?' she crooned down at Jemima. He wondered where she found the energy for that smile. 'As if I'd do that.'

The baby stared up at her intently, working noisily on her dummy.

'You know, Seb, you ought to go to bed. There's

no point in the both of us losing a good night's sleep.'

Not a chance. He wasn't leaving her to deal with this on her own *again*. Woman and child were ensconced on the sofa in the baby's room. He sat on the floor, resting back against it. He was hoping Eliza and the baby would drop off to sleep and then he'd watch over them—make sure the baby didn't roll off her lap or anything like that. At least then he'd feel as if he was pulling his weight.

He rubbed his nape. 'Do you think she's teething?'

'Babies don't usually start teething until they're six months. Her cheeks aren't pink and she's not rubbing at her mouth or pulling on her ears.'

'Then why…?' If he could find out what it was that was making Jemima cry, he'd set about fixing it. 'Should I call a doctor?'

She shook her head. 'I don't think it's anything physical—especially when she's so cheerful during the day. I mean, she's not hungry. Her nappy doesn't need changing. She doesn't have a temperature. And she stops crying whenever I pick her up.'

'So…comfort?'

She huffed out a long breath. 'Looks like it.'

'Then why won't she accept comfort from me?' It was unfair that Eliza had to bear the brunt of this.

'I suspect she will in a few days. Once she's more used to you. I suspect she's more familiar with women—or, at least, a woman—than men.'

He supposed that made sense.

Golden eyes met his. 'But I don't want to keep doing this. Sleepless nights are the pits.'

He couldn't blame her. But he wasn't sure how to help.

'I need a pram.'

He sat up a bit straighter. 'I told you to buy whatever you needed.' He winced at the glare she sent him. He probably deserved it. 'I'll organise one first thing in the morning.'

'Thank you.'

'You have a plan?'

She gave a hard nod. 'Jemima and I are going to spend a huge portion of tomorrow in the park…in the sunshine. I seem to recall that sunshine helps to regulate one's sleeping patterns.' Her brow crinkled again. 'Or is that an old wives' tale?'

For a moment she looked so disconsolate that all he wanted to do was buck up her spirits. 'It's not an old wives' tale. It's got something to do with melatonin.'

She stared at him as if he was speaking a foreign language.

'Daylight helps regulate one's body clock and melatonin is a hormone that makes us sleep well. They're related somehow. It has to do with our circadian rhythms.' He couldn't remember exactly how it all fitted together. 'I know because it's good for getting over jet lag too.' He made himself sound as confident and certain as he could—she looked in need of some certainty.

'Right. Good. It's spring. There's no better time for flooding this little body with as much natural daylight as I can than first thing in the morning. And I'm going to try and keep her awake as much as I reasonably can tomorrow—not let her sleep as much through the day as she has been.'

He lifted both hands and crossed his fingers.

'Which means she's going to be seriously grizzly come tomorrow evening.'

'I'll be here to help out.'

She shook her head. 'You need to focus on finding her mother. What's your plan?'

He shuffled upright a little more. 'I've thought about this from every angle.' He'd thought of little else...other than the dark circles under Eliza's eyes. 'I'm going to hire a private investigator. I know somebody discreet. He can start searching hospital records or the Department of Births, Deaths and Marriages for babies born in the last three to five months with the name Jemima.'

She raised an eyebrow. 'Do you know how many babies are born in the Greater London area alone in a single day?'

He had no idea but her expression told him it

was a lot. 'I have to start somewhere. Do you have a better plan?'

She looked as if she might say something, but she readjusted the baby in her arms instead. 'No,' she sighed.

'And I need to make a phone call.' He didn't want to ring Rhoda, but he had to. He couldn't hide from that fact any longer.

He pulled the phone from his pocket, but before he could bring up his list of contacts a hand fell on his shoulder. 'You can't call anyone at this time of night!'

He stared at the clock before shaking his head, trying to clear the mist that had him in its grip. 'No. I can't. What on earth am I thinking?'

A giggle shot out of her. 'If sunlight is good for jet lag then you might want to make a point of getting a good dose of the stuff tomorrow too.'

And then they were suddenly both laughing—hearty, break-the-tension laughter. Jemima spat her dummy out and laughed too. A sense of wellbeing he had no right to feeling flooded every cell of his body, making him feel lighter and more buoyant.

When their laughter eased to hiccups he flicked a glance at the clock. 'It was about this time in Australia when you phoned to inform me of *the emergency*.' His lips twitched upwards, and a low laugh left him. 'The tone of your voice! I'll never forget it.'

'I was…nonplussed.'

'You were riled.'

'Panicked,' she countered. 'I mean, who just leaves a baby on a stranger's desk? I…' She shook her head and then bit a hangnail. 'My sister has just found out that she's pregnant, you see, so babies have been on my mind lately.'

He turned to face her more fully. 'You have a sister?'

Watch your mouth! She needed to guard her tongue during these cosy 'wee hours of the morning' sessions. 'Yes.' It was pointless saying otherwise now.

He surveyed her with those grey eyes.

Despite the intermittently screaming baby, the atmosphere was remarkably easy, almost relaxed. She frowned. Was that a good thing?

'Is your sister happy about the baby?'

Liv's heart clenched. 'She's terrified.' She had no idea what Liz was going to do. But she sincerely hoped it wasn't something her sister would come to regret.

'Why?'

She stared down at the baby in her arms. 'It wasn't planned. She had a fling with a mystery man.' Which was so out of character for Liz it still made Liv's head spin. Not that she begrudged her sister a little fun, for letting her hair down for once and living a little. Liz deserved to be happy.

Except an unplanned pregnancy was a big thing. Single motherhood was a big thing. It was inordinately difficult—emotionally and financially—for a woman to raise a child on her own. And she wasn't sure Liz had any intention of doing so. Which begged the question—what on earth *was* Liz going to do?

Her stomach churned every time she thought about it.

'A mystery man?'

She recalled the dreamy look on Liz's face when she'd described him and couldn't help but smile. 'A tall, dark and handsome stranger, apparently. Their eyes met across a crowded room. You know the drill.'

'How old is your sister?'

Liv stiffened at the implicit criticism. 'Old enough not to deserve the condemnation in your voice!' She glared at him. 'Why is it OK for men to have flings and not women? She's not in a relationship with anyone. She works hard and meets her daily responsibilities. She wasn't hurting anyone.'

He dragged a hand down his face. 'You're right. I'm sorry.'

He stared at the baby she held, the baby who, to all intents and purposes, *looked* asleep. Previous experience warned Liv, though, that if she tried to put Jemima into her cot she'd wake with a start and scream the place down.

He turned to face her fully, his eyes serious and his mouth grim. 'She has to tell the father she's pregnant.'

He was projecting. Because he'd want to know if he ever fathered a child. He'd want to be involved in his child's life.

How can you possibly know that?

Easy-peasy—look how seriously he was taking his responsibility towards Jemima and her unknown mother...when he wasn't even sure if there was a link between them yet.

'She has to tell him,' he repeated.

She glanced back at him. He really had a bee in his bonnet about it. 'She's going to...just as soon as she can track him down.'

He'd started to subside against the sofa, but now he stiffened with an oath. 'That's why you requested leave, isn't it? You wanted to help her? Why didn't you say?'

She swallowed, a weight pressing down on her shoulders. 'We don't talk about personal things in the office.'

'I... No.' His shoulders slumped. 'You must think me some kind of ogre. If you need to go and support your sister you have my blessing. Take all the time you need.'

A lump filled her throat. Why did he have to be so darn decent? She couldn't speak so she merely raised an eyebrow and glanced down at Jemima.

He lifted a stubborn chin. 'I'll cope.'

That made her smile. He probably would but...
'I love my sister to bits, Seb. She's not just my sister. She's my best friend too. I'd do anything for her—*anything*. But this is something she needs to do on her own.'

'If you're sure.'

She wasn't sure about anything.

A silence descended. They didn't speak, both evidently lost in their own thoughts. And then Jemima twitched and started to stir.

Liv stared.

Oh!

'Seb, are you still awake?'

'Yes.'

'Recite something—a poem, a prayer, a song. I don't care what. Nothing bombastic. Something gentle.'

Without hesitation he recited the words to an Elvis Presley song. As he did, she watched the baby carefully. The twitching stopped and Jemima seemed to settle...to fall back into a deeper sleep.

'I think talking soothes her...lulls her. I think it's silence that she doesn't like.'

He crouched in front of them and recited another song. When he finished he stared into her eyes, his own wide and excited. 'I believe you've cracked the puzzle.'

He was so close she could feel his heat, and her

chest swelled at the admiration in his eyes. Then his gaze lowered to her lips and the grey in his eyes turned warm and smoky, the silver lights in them sparking and glittering. An answering pulse kicked to life in her throat—an ache, an overarching thirst, stretching through her. She stared at the beckoning breadth of his shoulders, and her arms and legs went catch-me weak. Heat flooded her every cell.

His eyes darkened to a smoky storm, but one corner of his mouth kinked upwards—a ragged edge full of wolfish satisfaction. He recognised her hunger...he revelled in it. And she need only give him one sign and he'd be more than happy to assuage it.

She snaked her tongue out to moisten parched lips. It'd be so easy to run her hands across those shoulders, to learn their strength and latent power, to dig her fingers into the muscled flesh and pull him closer. Her breath hitched and her lips parted on an involuntary sigh.

Temptation coiled around her in ever smaller circles, shackling her to her body's demands. She wanted him to kiss her. She wanted it more than she could remember ever wanting anything.

Her heart pounded so hard she was amazed the vibrations didn't wake the baby.

The baby...

She blinked.

Liz...

Hell!

Reefing her gaze from his, she stared doggedly down at Jemima and started inanely reciting nursery rhymes. Her heart had led her astray once before. She wasn't giving it the chance to do so again.

Seb wasn't Brent, but he came from a different world to her, and it was just too…fraught.

Too foolish.

She'd lost too much last time.

Without another word, Sebastian rose and left the room.

She touched her lips to the baby's head, and tried to slow the pounding of her pulse. 'Oh, Jemima, there's a whole can of worms I need to keep a lid on here. I can't mess this up.' Messing up was not an option.

Liv woke to find sunlight flooding Jemima's room. She sat up and massaged the crick in her neck before pushing aside the blanket someone had placed over her. Sebastian?

She rolled her eyes. Obviously it was Sebastian. There wasn't anyone else here.

She rested back and pulled in a breath. It was so blissfully quiet.

She glanced at the clock and then did a double take. It was after nine o'clock!

She counted off on her fingers. That meant she'd had somewhere between five and six hours' sleep.

Thank you, God!

She was tempted to curl up and sleep for another two or three hours—she'd bet Sebastian wouldn't mind—but curiosity propelled her to her feet. Where were Seb and the baby? And how had he managed to keep Jemima quiet for so long?

She padded downstairs in her bare feet, and out to the kitchen with its attached conservatory. Seb was sitting at the table with Jemima on his lap and they were both eating…

Oh, God, eating! Was Jemima ready for solids yet?

She tried to ask the question, but as she rounded the table and caught sight of Seb properly, her throat closed over and nothing but a garbled sound emerged. Seb had changed out of his business trousers and button-down shirt and wore nothing but a pair of well-worn, low-slung jeans and a tight white T-shirt that outlined every lean, hard inch of him. The man was ripped and cut in ways she'd not imagined.

In ways she'd *tried* not to imagine.

And the reality made her mouth dry. She couldn't look away.

Jemima's squeal and her waving arms broke the spell. Her evident excitement at seeing Liv filled her with warmth. She swooped in to give the baby a kiss, and then backed up again as the scent of hot, spicy man flooded her nostrils. She had the foresight to grab the jar of food Seb was feeding Jemima as she backpedalled, to read its label.

'Baby custard…for babies of three months,' he said, reaching over to take the jar back from her. 'She loves it.'

He fed Jemima a spoonful and she smacked her lips in evident enjoyment.

'You can't blame her. The stuff tastes great.' He popped a teaspoon of custard into his mouth, half closing his eyes in relish before dipping the spoon back into the custard and holding it out to her. 'You've got to try this stuff. It's out of this world.'

For a moment she was tempted, and then she frowned. Had she entered an alternative reality? Where had Liz's staid, remote boss gone? This scene—sexy man and cute baby, happy smiles and easy rapport…*ooh*, it was too attractive, too beguiling. She couldn't allow herself to get sucked into it.

Acid burned her stomach. Seb might not be twenty years older than her…as Brent had been, but he'd still be seven or eight years older. He was a man of the world, and there was little doubt he had far more experience than she.

And he was a lord to boot!

You know what happens when mere mortals fraternise with the gods.

Not that he was a god.

But she *was* a mere mortal. And she'd never fit into the life of someone like Sebastian Tyrell.

'No?' He held the spoon up a little higher, a teasing smile playing across those lips that had tempted her last night, and still tempted her today.

No! And she couldn't let him get sucked into this craziness either. He looked more than capable of looking after himself, but...

He was grateful to her. He trusted her. *And she was lying to him.*

'Ah.' His face cleared. 'Not human until after coffee and a shower. I remember. There's coffee in the pot on the hotplate over there.'

She drank her first cup black, and in silence, content to watch man and baby. They made a pretty contrast—the baby so small and fair and innocent, and the man so big and strong and—

Stop staring!

She drained the contents of her mug, set it on the table, and opened her mouth.

'Nope.' He pointed back the way she'd come. 'Go and take that shower. I'll put a fresh pot on to brew. It'll be ready by the time you're done, then you can drink another mug and then you'll be human.'

The kindness and warmth in his eyes made her chest burn. Without another word she turned and fled.

She stood under the stinging spray of the shower and recited over and over, *'Don't mess this up. Don't mess this up'* until her pulse returned to something approaching a normal rate.

She scrubbed herself dry with a soft, fluffy towel that caressed her skin rather than abraded it, all the while trying to ignore the sparks, the aches and yearnings that ebbed and flowed through her. Things between her and Sebastian Tyrell were becoming far too cosy far too quickly.

She wished they hadn't agreed to first names. She wished they'd maintained the formality of surnames—of Mr and Ms.

She finished dressing and then sat on the side of her bed, drawing in a deep breath. Bonding over the baby had evidently broken down barriers with an ease that wasn't the norm. Combine it with sleep deprivation…

She let the breath out slowly. But she was no longer sleep-deprived. They'd do their best to get Jemima sleeping through the night in four-hourly blocks, and she'd insist on them taking shifts—he could take the first half of the night and she'd take the second. Or vice versa.

No more cosy chats in the wee small hours. And no more sharing confidences. In fact, if she could get Jemima to sleep in four-hourly blocks, she wouldn't need Seb's help during the night at all.

She shot to her feet. It was time to badger him to start searching for Jemima's mother in earnest. That'd keep them out of each other's hair.

When she returned to the kitchen she found a steaming mug of coffee waiting for her, a small but sweet porcelain jug standing near by—probably a priceless heirloom—filled with milk. She carefully—*very carefully*—poured milk into her mug.

He smiled as if satisfied with something and eased back in his chair. She took a sip—such good coffee!—and he said, 'How do you feel?'

She wanted to laugh and say, *Human*, but a voice inside her intoned *Distance* in such stern tones she didn't. 'Thank you for letting me sleep.'

His eyes narrowed a fraction. 'You're welcome. You'd earned it.'

'How did you keep Jemima quiet?' She winced as a sudden thought hit her. 'Tell me I didn't sleep through the wailing and gnashing of teeth?'

He shook his head. 'Audio books did the trick. Both you and Jemima slept through E.M. Forster's *A Room With a View*.'

They had?

'Or, at least, a portion of it.'

He grinned. 'I'm saving the rest for tonight.'

It took all of her strength not to grin back.

'Though now we've a selection to choose from as I've bought a whole range of children's audio books. Mind you, I suspect it's the vocal rhythms rather than the content of what's being said that Jemima appreciates. I also bought a crate of baby custard, and the pram you requested.'

She glanced in the direction he pointed to find a gleaming pram standing there. How had she not noticed it earlier? It looked like the highest of high-end prams! 'How...how did you make that happen so quickly?'

'Online shopping. London. Express delivery.'

She'd bet that express delivery had cost him a pretty packet. 'Excellent. Thank you.'

His eyes narrowed a fraction more. 'You're welcome.'

'So that's Jemima and me taken care of for the day—sunshine in the park. What's your plan?'

'I thought I'd help you with the baby.'

Her heart clenched, but she hardened it. 'I don't need help with the baby.'

He stared at her, his mouth slightly open, and then he snapped it into a tight line and his face shuttered closed and she'd never felt like a bigger heel in her life.

She forced herself to go on. 'Have you hired your private investigator yet?'

His chin came up, all stone and disdain. 'I have.'

'And have you made your phone call?'

'Yes.'

She moistened suddenly dry lips. 'So...what did your father say?'

He frowned as if she'd lost him, the hauteur momentarily falling away. 'It wasn't my father that I rang.'

CHAPTER FOUR

Not his father? Then who—?

A woman?

None of your business.

She glanced at Jemima playing happily with her baby gym in the light-filled conservatory—and she offered up a silent prayer of thanks for all of that light—but… While it might not be her business, it was certainly Jemima's business. And as soon as she'd agreed to look after the baby, Jemima's business had become her business.

She glanced back at Seb, who surveyed her steadily, although no compelling smile now flickered in his eyes, no shared camaraderie softened the firm lines of his mouth.

She missed that. She wished she didn't, but she did.

She forced back an apology, and a teasing quip designed to open the way for their previous easiness again. It wouldn't do. She forced herself to concentrate on the conversation rather than her sense of loss.

He'd rung a woman? And yet she'd believed him when he'd sworn that none of his ex-girlfriends could be Jemima's mother. Maybe she shouldn't have, but she did. There was something innately honest about Seb. He was a man you could trust.

Unlike you.

She pushed the thought away. She might be lying to him, but she was also helping him. They mightn't precisely cancel each other out, but it had to help balance the scales a little bit.

She moistened her lips. 'Did your phone call give you any clues as to the identity of Jemima's parents?'

'No.'

She waited but he didn't expand further. Fine, she'd just have to come right out with it. 'Don't you think you need to speak to your father?'

One of his hands tightened to a fist. When he saw her staring at it, he opened it and started drumming his fingers against the table. 'My father can't be trusted.'

The glare he sent her should've charred her on the spot. *Whoa!* So this was the grumpy boss her sister had told her about. She lifted her chin and glared right back.

He slammed a finger to the table between them. 'What do you want from me?'

'I want you to find Jemima's parents!'

'No.' His glare intensified, his eyes narrowing on her face. 'You're angry with me and I want to know why.'

* * *

'You're talking rot.'

But her gaze slid away as she said it and something in his chest clenched up hard and tight.

'I'm not the least bit cross with you. But I do want this situation sorted.'

While he'd been looking forward to spending the day in the park with her and Jemima? He was a certifiable idiot!

He stilled, recalling the near panic that had flicked across her face when he'd told her he meant to spend the day helping her with the baby. He remembered that moment last night when they'd stared at each other with such naked hunger he'd almost combusted on the spot. A tiger had woken inside him and roared to full wakefulness. He'd been about to kiss her. And she'd wanted him to.

He'd been ready to take everything she offered him. He'd wanted her to offer *everything*. He'd been tempted to seduce her into mindless compliance so they could both lose themselves to the pleasure they could give each other, regardless of the consequences.

His lips twisted. Like father, like son.

He had to back away from that edge *fast*. He deliberately brought Rhoda's face to his mind.

'You're concerned about that moment last night when I nearly kissed you. It's playing on your mind.'

She opened her mouth as if to deny his words, but shut it again, her eyes clouded and troubled.

'It's been playing on mine too.' He leaned across the table towards her. 'You have my word that you've nothing to fear.' He kept his gaze, his attention, on her eyes. Not on her mouth, or the beguiling line of her throat, or that amazing hair. 'I promise that I will not try to kiss you or do anything else the least inappropriate.'

Her hands twisted together. 'It's just… You're still my boss.'

'And you don't want history repeating itself.' She'd trusted him enough to confide that, and her trust deserved a better repayment than him drooling all over her.

She drooled back.

That was beside the point!

'Seb, you're nothing like my previous…boss.'

That eased the burning in his soul a fraction.

'But I still don't want to have a workplace romance.'

'It's a recipe for disaster,' he agreed.

'Listen, we were both tired and it was the small hours of the night and—'

He gave a laugh, but it lacked mirth. 'That's nonsense and we both know it.'

Her eyes widened. Her throat bobbed as she swallowed.

'We can at least be honest with ourselves. I find

you very desirable and I don't think the attraction is completely one-sided.'

'Oh!' She bit her lip and stared at him with deer-in-the-headlights eyes.

'But, being aware of it, we can take care to avoid fanning the flames...to tread with caution. Agreed?'

'Agreed.'

But her voice came out high and squeaky, and the need to kiss her roared through him. He gritted his teeth and clenched his hands...and waited for it to pass.

And kept right on waiting.

He unclenched his jaw a fraction. 'Yesterday you confided in me. Let me now make my position clear too. Like you, I've been burned by an... unhealthy relationship.'

Her throat tightened as she swallowed. 'Unhealthy?'

He had no intention of confiding the details of the betrayal he'd suffered at Rhoda's hands. He refused to relive the humiliation, the shame...the *degradation*. 'I won't bore you with the details. Suffice it to say that the aristocrat thing has a tendency to attract the worst kind of person. I have no desire to form any kind of lasting relationship. I have no desire to perpetuate the species or to keep my line running.'

Her throat bobbed once, twice…three times. 'Wow. Right. OK.'

'I choose my liaisons…carefully.'

She folded her arms, her eyes going hard. 'You prefer to fraternise with women of your own class.'

He opened his mouth to debunk her theory as snobbish rubbish, but closed it again. He thrust out his jaw. He didn't need to justify himself to her. Besides, if she thought that then maybe she'd feel safe. 'I refuse to risk my business relationships for the sake of scratching a temporary itch,' he said, deliberately crude. 'Sleeping with my secretaries would mean having to hire a new secretary every time the current one flounced off in a huff when she realised I meant it when I said I'd never marry.'

She blinked.

'Good help is harder to get than a good—'

'I get your point, Mr Tyrell! You don't need to explain it in any further detail.'

He tried not to wince at that *Mr Tyrell*. But the automatic way it came out of her mouth made him think that maybe, once this was all over, things would return to normal.

The thought should make him feel happier.

He lifted his chin. 'I just want us on the same page. I don't want you worried that I'll attempt to seduce you. You have my word that I won't.'

She laughed, but he didn't understand why.

'Don't worry, I believe you. And I appreciate your frankness, Seb.'

He had a feeling that she said his name to let him know she wasn't outraged at his revelation, that she didn't hold it against him. But he had to fight back a groan at the sound of it on her lips. The rightness of it.

'So I'm going to be equally frank.'

Dear God. How could this conversation get any franker?

'It still appears obvious to me that you need to speak to your father.'

Acid burned in his gut, tempering his lust.

'If he's the key to this mystery, as you suspect, then why are you delaying confronting him?'

The last of his desire dissolved. He shoved away from the table on the pretext of pouring himself more coffee. He held the coffee pot up towards her in a silent question, but she shook her head.

She continued to stare at him with relentless eyes. 'Well?'

He took a measured sip, leaning back against a kitchen bench as if the cares of the world weren't trying to pound him into the ground. 'I think it'll be best to wait and see what the private investigator turns up.'

'That could take days!'

'What is it you're really worried about?'

She shot to her feet, slamming her hands to her

hips. 'What I want to know is why *you're* not more worried? In not reporting Jemima's situation, I suspect we're both skating on the wrong side of the law.'

It was unconscionable to have put her in this position.

'But apart from my fears about the legalities, there's a woman out there who obviously felt so far at the end of her tether she abandoned her baby to strangers. For Jemima's sake we need to find her and help her.'

'You're putting a singularly positive spin on it.' He shifted, trying to get comfortable against the bench. 'Jemima's mother could be a drug addict who'll contact us soon enough with menaces— demanding money.'

'If someone in your family is Jemima's father, her mother is entitled to financial aid in the shape of child support. Do you know how financially difficult it is for single mothers in this country? Do you know that across all developed countries in the world single mothers are among the poorest members of society?'

How did she know that? And then he recalled her sister's predicament. He suddenly saw how personal this situation must feel to her.

'And they can't win! If they have a full-time job they're bad mothers for not spending enough time with their child. But if they decide to be stay-at-home mums they're vilified for being welfare queens and a strain on society. Single fathers aren't viewed in the same way. They aren't subjected to the same prejudices. No!' She paced up and down, waving her hands in the air. 'They're patted on the back for going above and beyond. How can it be considered *above and beyond* when it's your own child? This world is set up to benefit and protect men, at the expense of women. It makes me so mad!'

Jemima gave a loud cry and Eliza immediately dropped down on the quilted rug beside the baby, all smiles, making Jemima laugh with the aid of a teddy bear and a silly voice.

His gut clenched up tight. 'Is there anything I can do to help your sister?'

Her shoulders slumped. 'I'm not blaming you for society's ills, Seb. I'm not saying they're your fault or of your making.'

'I know that.' But it didn't change the fact that he benefited—unknowingly—from the way society was set up. 'But if there's anything I can do to help, then I want to.'

She glanced up at him and he couldn't read the expression in her eyes—it was a mixture of warmth, sadness, and feeling all at sea. 'You can't help my sister, but you can help the poor woman who left Jemima in your care.'

Her words sucker-punched him. He had to brace

his hands on his knees for a moment to catch his breath. 'I haven't seen or spoken to my father in two years.'

Her mouth fell open. She snapped it shut. 'I'm sorry. I didn't know there was a rift.'

'You wouldn't.' He straightened. 'It's not a story that ever made the papers.'

She pursed her lips and then lifted the baby onto her lap. Woman and child stared at him and myriad emotions crowded his chest. He lifted his gaze to the ceiling and counted to ten before glancing back at her. 'What? Out with it.'

She grimaced. 'It's going to sound hard and—'

'I'm discovering, Eliza, that you have a propensity for uttering hard truths.'

'I don't mean to hurt your feelings.'

Those golden eyes were so wide and so worried he found himself biting back the beginnings of a smile. 'Understood and appreciated.'

She grimaced again. 'It's just that I don't believe your pride should hold much weight in the face of Jemima's predicament.'

Ouch!

'Look at her, Seb.' She ran her hand over the crown of the baby's head as if he needed further convincing. 'She's so innocent…and so lovely. She deserves only good things, the best that life can offer.' She pulled in a breath. 'She deserves better than this.'

He wanted to point out that the baby currently had a roof over her head, food in her belly and two people at her beck and call, but it wasn't what she meant.

She was right. They needed to clear up this mystery and put things to rights as quickly as they could—for the baby's sake.

But...

'You don't seem to understand. Confronting my father will do no good.' Everything inside of him went cold. 'Hector is a liar and a cheat without an honest bone in his body. He won't tell me—or you—the truth. The sight of a baby won't move him. There are reasons we're estranged. Good reasons.' He and his father were done. For good.

She stared at him for a long moment, her eyes cloudy, and then rose with Jemima in her arms. 'Why don't we go for that walk?'

'I didn't think you wanted—'

'We're making a plan or, at least, trying to find a way forward. That's good...useful. We may as well make it in the sun in the pretty gardens.'

And just like that she made him feel less alone. It should've been impossible. And he probably shouldn't have revelled in the sensation, not even for a single second. But for a moment he simply couldn't help it.

Less than ten minutes later they were strolling in the park. It was a perfect spring day—warm with blues skies, the occasional ripple of white cloud drifting high above. The gardens were bursting with colour and blooms. Tulips in myriad colours all vied to out-display each other. The scent of freshly mown grass and cherry blossom filled the air. Everything was warm, fragrant…idyllic.

Liv halted the pram to adjust the little sunhat Jemima wore and the hood of the pram to make sure the baby's face was properly shaded. 'I want her to get lots of light, but I don't want her to burn.' She straightened and glanced across at him. 'Is pushing a pram unmanly?'

'I have no idea.' And, frankly, he didn't care if it was. He took her place pushing the pram while she walked alongside staring at the cherry trees, the gardens…the squirrels. He sensed her mind racing, and he wondered how much of her surroundings she actually saw. He didn't interrupt her. He simply kept walking and waited.

'Seb?'

'Yes?'

She swung to face him. 'Look, I'm not going to ask why you haven't spoken to your father in so long.'

Ice tripped down his spine and a vice gripped his temples. Just as well, as he had no intention of enlightening her.

'But you obviously believe it's possible that he's either Jemima's father or grandfather.'

He stared straight ahead, but could feel the heat of her gaze. It seared his flesh. 'I don't believe for a single moment that my father will make any such admission.'

She didn't say anything and his flesh burned brighter and hotter.

'Eliza?'

'Yes?'

'Are you staring at me?'

He felt the release from her gaze as she swung forward again. He momentarily closed his eyes at the respite.

'You went all icy,' she murmured.

'Would you prefer I worked myself into a passion?'

She hesitated a beat too long. 'No!' The word emerged too breathy, too full of anticipation.

An anticipation that couldn't be explored. He ground his teeth together.

'There was an incident two and a half years ago.' He pulled in a breath, felt his nostrils flare as his stomach started to churn. He glanced at her. 'You understand this is just between you and me.'

She crossed her heart.

He turned his gaze back to the front. 'A young man came forward claiming Hector was his biological father. He was the son of one of our former housemaids.'

'And?'

'My parents threw him out of the house, with various insults and thinly veiled threats.'

Her breath hitched but he refused to turn and look at her again. 'And you?' she whispered.

'His story seemed…creditable. So I went after him.' His lips twisted. Oh, yes, it had been all too plausible. All his adult life Hector had used his charm and position to take whatever he wanted from whomever he wanted—including the sexual favours of his staff—before tossing them aside without thought or care. 'We had a DNA comparison done.'

'Oh! Did…did your parents know what you were doing?'

'Yes.' There'd been the most God-awful row. It was his first glimpse of Rhoda's true colours. He should've heeded them then.

'Well, good for you!'

From the corner of his eye he saw her plant her hands on her hips and give a decisive nod. She seemed to grow taller and for some reason it made him want to smile.

'So…the results? Was he your half-brother?'

'No.' Acid coated his tongue. 'More's the pity. I liked him.'

'Oh!' She stared up at him with throbbing eyes before reaching out and touching his arm, her fingers wrapping about his wrist, her eyes filling with warmth and sympathy.

The action slid in beneath his guard. And then the warmth of her hand registered and a pulse quickened through him, spreading heat and havoc.

He wanted to pull her to him. He wanted to shake her off.

He wanted to stop *feeling*.

'I'm sorry.'

They'd stopped and he forced his feet forward again. He told himself he was glad when her hand dropped away. 'My parents weren't. They were delighted at the outcome.' They'd crowed about their victory. 'But that was the moment I became aware that I could have several half-siblings I knew nothing about.'

'Did you ask them—your parents?'

Of course he'd asked them.

'Of course you asked them!' she said, echoing his unspoken words. 'But they refused to tell you anything—right?'

Exactly.

They both walked in silence for a while. 'I take it your mother wouldn't be of any help?'

'None whatsoever. She's as bad as Hector.'

'What about staff—do you have any allies there?'

He did. Brownie and George had been at Tyrell Hall his entire life. But they didn't believe in gossiping about their betters. If only he could make them see that they were worth ten Lord and Lady Tyrells.

'What about old records…diaries…photo albums?'

Would either of his parents have been foolish enough to keep records that might incriminate them, that would make them financially responsible for someone else?

He pursed his lips. It wasn't inconceivable. His father in particular was reckless. It was a possibility. A remote one, but a possibility all the same.

'Seb?'

He shrugged. 'The odds are slim.'

'But better than what we have at the moment. Where would such things be kept? Here in London or at your Lincolnshire estate?'

'Lincolnshire.'

'Then…what are we waiting for?'

He halted halfway down the avenue of cherry trees. Here and there white blossom floated down through the air. Everything smelled fresh and sweet.

'You want to go to Lincolnshire?' He thought she'd been trying to get rid of him.

She huffed out a breath. '*Want* might be stretching the point a little. But I'm bullying you into finding Jemima's mother and it seems a little cold-hearted to send you off on your own.'

She wanted to give him moral support? For a

moment he was speechless. He couldn't remember the last time anyone had tried to be so supportive of him.

Which was his own fault. He rarely gave anyone the chance. But…

'What?' She pushed her hair back from her face.

He started when he realised he'd been staring, forced his feet forward again. 'You haven't bullied me into anything. You simply pointed out—correctly—that I was dragging my feet. You've no need to feel guilty.'

She bit the side of her thumb and sent him a look that seemed far from reassured. 'Two heads are better than one; four hands are better than two. And I might be able to help in other ways too.'

It took a force of will, but he kept his gaze on the path ahead. The avenue of cherry trees with their spectacular blossom paled in comparison to the woman beside him. Every cell in his body strained towards her. 'Such as?'

'Babies catch at people's hearts. The sight of Jemima might make somebody talk or confide in us.'

'You're a romantic, you know that?'

'I am not!'

She looked personally affronted at the idea and it made him laugh. For the briefest moment it made him feel young.

'And…' She raised a reluctant shoulder. 'There

are other less salubrious tactics we can resort to if needs be.'

'Such as?'

'Gossip.'

His stomach curdled.

'There are bound to be staff on the estate who've been there a long time…who might be able to provide us with a clue or two. Or neighbours or tradespeople.'

He stared down into the pram at the tiny baby. *How much am I going to be asked to sacrifice on your behalf, little one?*

'I see what you're driving at. You think that if you accompany me as Jemima's nanny it'll give you an inside track on any downstairs gossip.'

'It's a possibility, isn't it? It could at least be worth a try, don't you think?'

She didn't understand the ugliness she could uncover. Nausea made his stomach rebel and his head spin. He had to stop and brace his arms against the pram, concentrate on taking deep, cleansing breaths to keep it at bay.

A hand on his back sent warmth filtering into his veins, making the nausea recede. But replaced it with an ache that he dared not assuage.

'Seb, you're evidently not feeling well. Let's go back. You can lie down and—'

He captured her other hand in his and tugged her so close her perfume rose around him and he could see each individual eyelash—she smelled of gardenias and jam. 'Eliza, my parents have done some ugly things in their lifetimes. I've spent my adult life trying to make amends.'

The hand on his back moved to rest against his cheek. 'Oh, Seb, I'm so sorry. And here I am asking you to discover more potential awfulness.'

He needed some distance because he was in danger of breaking his promise and kissing her. He stepped back until her hand dropped away. 'If you come to Tyrell Hall with me I need to ask a favour of you.'

She stared at him wordlessly and then nodded. 'OK.'

'Whatever gossip you hear, whatever ugly things you learn, I need you to promise that you'll not go to the Press with the story.'

Her head rocked back. 'I'd never do such a thing! You have my word.'

Some of the tension drained from him. 'Thank you. You have to understand it's not my parents I want to protect, but the people they've hurt or taken advantage of.'

'I'll sign a waiver or contract or whatever to that effect. I've no desire to profit from this situation. I just want to see Jemima safe and settled, and—'

'I know. And I trust you.'

Shadowed eyes met his.

'Your word is good enough for me. I don't need you to sign anything.'

She glanced away. 'When do we leave for Lincolnshire?'

He wondered if she was already regretting her offer to accompany him. He turned the pram for home. 'How soon can you be ready?'

The closer they drew to Lincolnshire, the graver Seb became. The silence that had been mostly companionable—broken here and there with pockets of conversation—grew tight and tense.

Was he worried about what they might uncover once they started digging?

Of course he's worried!

Liv stared at the hands clenched about the steering wheel—those white knuckles—and wanted to fill the silence with chatter in an effort to distract him and ease his worries, if only temporarily.

But she didn't trust herself to chatter without giving Liz and herself away. For heaven's sake, she'd told him her sister was expecting a baby! What on earth would he think when in a week or so's time she—well, Liz, but he'd think it was her—told him she was pregnant too? Would he buy the coincidence?

She'd been meaning to keep a detailed journal outlining events as they happened and all of the things she and Seb talked about, but she'd yet to start it. Jemima had taken up all her time. Liz would need to know it all. Just thinking about the explanations, and accompanying justifications she'd feel compelled to add, left her feeling exhausted.

What on earth had she been thinking, offering to accompany *her sister's boss* to Lincolnshire? Why on earth hadn't she stopped to think for once? Being as far away from Seb as possible—and separate counties would've been perfect—would have made things so much simpler. Not to mention easier.

But the look on his face when he'd spoken about his parents... It had grabbed her heart and squeezed until she'd barely had breath left. He'd looked so *alone*.

She rubbed a hand across her chest. She was forcing him to delve into his parents' past—a course of action he had no appetite for—to poke a monster—maybe multiple monsters—that was probably better off left undisturbed. And she hated it! She hated being responsible for bringing that haunted, stony expression to his eyes.

Her phone buzzed as a text came through. *Liz!*

So sorry. I need a few more days. Please say you'll keep covering for me.

She texted back.

No prob. On way to Lincolnshire. Trying to track baby's mother.

What?

The word beamed out at her like an accusation.

How is your mission going?

She quickly sent the question to get her sister's mind off the predicament Liv had landed them in.

There was a long interval before her sister finally texted back.

I'll call you later.

Liv winced and shoved her phone back into her handbag, tried to slow the pounding of her heart. Was she making an utter hash of things here?

She bit her lip. How was Liz really doing? She'd said she needed a few more days? Did that mean she'd found her tall, dark mystery man? She wriggled, rubbing her shoulders against the plush leather of her seat. If she had…and they'd liked each other enough to spend five steamy days together…maybe—

'Is everything OK?'

She started when Seb spoke. 'Everything's fine,' she lied.

He sent her a brief, narrow-eyed glance. 'Regretting your offer to accompany me already?'

'No!' She shuffled upright. And then grimaced at the look he sent her—the man was too perceptive by half. 'A little,' she admitted. 'I don't have much experience with fraught family politics. My family is lovely.'

'You see a lot of them?'

'I do.'

The stark whiteness of his knuckles eased, so she continued. 'My parents live in Berkshire. They're both schoolteachers. Mum is Australian and they met when Dad was there on holiday.'

'She came back with him?'

That made her laugh. 'Absolutely not. She refused to relocate and upend her life on the basis of only two weeks' acquaintance. So he stayed and got a posting to a local high school there. When he'd proven his devotion, and she was sure of her feelings for him, they married before moving to England.'

'That's equal parts romantic and sensible.'

'They're devoted to each other...and to my sister and me.'

'Where does you sister live?'

'London...out towards Watford.'

'What does she do?'

The more relaxed his hands became on the steering wheel, the tighter the knot in her chest. 'She's an office temp.' It felt innately deceitful to speak of herself in the third person like this to him. *It is deceitful. You're going to hell.*

She bit back a sigh. She'd do anything for Liz, even this.

'She doesn't have a permanent position?'

'She doesn't want one. She likes the freedom temping gives her. And she says the money is good.' The truth was Liv didn't have the heart to settle for the monotony of a single day-in, day-out job.

'But there are no benefits in temping—no holiday leave or sick leave…maternity leave.'

'She, um…also designs jewellery.' Liv had needed a creative outlet when she'd dropped out of art school…after Brent. She loved working with silver and semi-precious stones, but it didn't come close to filling the gap left by painting and sketching.

'Is she any good?'

She shrugged. 'I've no idea.'

'Will it support her once the baby comes?'

'Seb, this is none of your business.'

He grimaced. 'Sorry. Focusing on your family is a more attractive proposition than focusing on mine.'

For him, maybe. Not for her.

He gestured at the windscreen. 'You'll get your first glimpse of Tyrell Hall when we top the rise up ahead.'

They'd left the motorway over twenty minute ago, and were now winding their way through low green hills on a single carriageway. Everything looked lush and gorgeous.

'To your left,' he said.

She looked and her jaw dropped. 'Oh, my God! It's massive, huge…enormous. It looks like something straight out of an Austen novel! And I've loved Austen since…*forever*!'

CHAPTER FIVE

TYRELL HALL SAT amid rolling green fields. A large number of outbuildings trailed out to its right, but it was the hall itself that held Liv's gaze…and her awe. In gorgeous grey stone, Tyrell Hall preened with an unselfconscious acknowledgement of its own grace and grandeur. For the briefest of moments her fingers ached for her sketchpad and charcoals.

But while the hall was more than aware of its charm, the grey stone and elegant lines were both weathered and warm rather than cold and uninviting. It stood three storeys high with two wings branching out either side, creating a U-shape that formed a large central courtyard. A fountain with frolicking Greek-style nymphs held pride of place in the centre. White-gravelled, rose-lined paths radiated out from it in eight different directions.

Just…wow!

She pointed to the main building. 'How old?'

Seb stared at it with shadows in his eyes and she realised that, rather than a beautiful historic building, he saw ghosts. Unhappy ghosts. She bit her lip. Evidently, growing up here hadn't been a happy adventure.

Not the house's fault. But still…

'It dates from the sixteenth century.'

'It's really beautiful.'

He blinked as if coming back to the present. 'You think so?'

'Absolutely!' She wanted to remove those shadows. 'Seb, regardless of anything else, empirically your house is amazing—graceful, elegant, not to mention historical...and just plain gorgeous!'

He stared at her with such evident disbelief she had to reach behind to scratch an itch between her shoulder blades. 'At least that's what my artist's eye tells me.'

'You have an artist's eye?'

'I do. A very good one.' Even if her fingers didn't want to work any more. 'Still, I understand that a house may be one thing, while its inhabitants are the polar opposite.'

He stared back at the house. 'It *is* considered rather fine in most circles,' he murmured as if only just remembering that fact. 'I...it's been a while since I looked at it properly. Sorry.'

He sent her a half-apologetic smile that twisted her heart.

'I'm afraid one takes it all for granted after a while.'

She didn't believe he took any of this for granted—not for a moment.

A sudden, rather awful thought struck her. She swallowed as they pushed out of the car. 'Seb?'

'Mmm?'

'Your parents don't still live here, do they?'

He physically recoiled from her. 'No!'

'Sorry.' She tried to swallow her wince. 'The house is so big I thought that maybe they lived in one wing and you lived in another and never the twain shall meet.'

He shook his head, those shadows alive and dangerous. 'No. This all belongs to me now.'

She didn't ask him how. It was none of her business. But he really needed to start making some happy memories here to shake away those ghosts from his past.

'Hector and Marjorie live in Monte Carlo.'

'Good.'

He raised an eyebrow. 'Good?'

She lifted the baby carrier out. 'It means I won't have to run into them, which therefore means I won't have to give them a piece of my mind.'

He laughed. It wasn't a deep belly laugh, more a quiet chuckle, but Liv counted it as a win.

Twelve wide stone steps led up to a grand portico. A portly middle-aged woman dressed in black stood waiting with an ominously straight back at the double-door entrance.

'Brownie!'

'Master Sebastian.'

Seb's grin of greeting, and the other woman's

smile, the way they embraced, dispelled Liv's trepidation.

'Brownie, I'd like you to meet my office manager-cum-nanny, Eliza Gilmour.' He turned towards Liv and his lips twitched. 'Also known as Mary Poppins.'

Oh, those lips could do seriously dangerous things to a woman's blood pressure.

Brownie pressed her lips together in evident disapproval, though her eyes seemed to smile in spite of her. 'I'm Mrs Brown.'

Liv found herself smiling too. She gestured to the baby. 'And this is Jemima, who is currently blissfully asleep.'

Brownie glanced at the baby and then at Seb with a question in her eyes.

Seb shrugged and glanced back at Liv. 'Brownie—Mrs Brown—has been the housekeeper here at Tyrell Hall for as long as I can remember. She made sure I was fed and clothed, and let me know when I stepped out of line.'

She saw it all in an instant. Mrs Brown had been Seb's surrogate family. She'd done what she could to prevent a small boy from feeling too lonely in this enormous house. She'd been someone the younger Seb could turn to for comfort and a measure of security.

'I'm *really* pleased to meet you, Mrs Brown.'

Liv meant every word and the sharp look the

housekeeper sent her told Liv she knew it too. She didn't know if that was a good thing or not. But one thing was clear—if she didn't stop revealing her personal feelings so unreservedly, she'd be making things a lot harder for Liz when she returned.

'Excuse me, Ms Gilmour, but I've never been one for taking nonsense. Master Sebastian, will you kindly tell me what you're doing with a baby?'

'It's a long story…and we're weary travellers in much need of sustenance.'

She chuckled. 'Come on in with you both. George!'

A man appeared and he and Seb shook hands, big smiles lighting their faces.

'Tush, enough of that! George, bring in the bags and garage the car.' As George left, she turned back to them. 'If you'd like to rest yourselves in the green sitting room, I'll—'

'Not a chance, Brownie. We're coming into the kitchen with you.'

Liv followed Seb and Mrs Brown out towards the back of the house and learned that George was Mrs Brown's husband—and, yes, his lumbago was doing just fine thank you very much, especially now he'd started seeing a new man in the village for some fancy kind of newfangled massage therapy—and that, between the two of them, they kept the place running.

Liv stopped dead when they came to the doorway of the kitchen. Something inside her chest expanded. The room was generously proportioned with an old-fashioned cast-iron cooker set into one wall alongside a more up-to-date oven. The stone-flagged floors might've been cold if not for a large blue and white rug that looked completely at home beneath an enormous wooden table, which had pride of place in the centre of the room.

She started when she realised the conversation had stopped and both her employer and the housekeeper were staring at her.

'Is everything all right, Ms Gilmour?'

'Everything is perfect.' She stepped into the room and gestured around. 'I think I've just fallen in love.'

'Aye.' Mrs Brown's eyes lit with warmth. 'It's the nicest kitchen I've ever worked in.'

'It the only kitchen you've ever worked in,' was Seb's wry reply.

It was nice seeing him in these surroundings, seeing him so at home with himself and the people here. Everyone deserved a place where they could feel at home.

She set the baby down, recalling the shadows in his eyes when they'd first arrived. At least they hadn't reappeared here in the kitchen. She glanced around again and it occurred to her that this might be the only room in the entire house where he did feel so unabashedly at home.

The thought burned through her, making her hands clench. She flexed her fingers. He worked from here, which meant he had to have an office somewhere near by. He'd have made that his own too. There had to be at least two rooms in this sprawling mansion he felt at home in, right?

Mrs Brown planted two steaming mugs on the table along with a plate of still-warm date scones. She pointed at Seb, and then the coffee and scones, and then a chair. 'Now you can start filling me in on this long story of yours.'

With a twist of his lips, Seb motioned Liv to a chair before taking the one next to her. She drank coffee and ate a scone as he told the housekeeper all about the events of the past few days.

'Well, now, this is a pickle and there's no denying it.'

'Any thoughts?'

Seb reached for a scone, his hands steady, but Liv sensed the tension in him.

Mrs Brown shook her head, glancing at him and then at the still sleeping Jemima. 'I can't abide gossip or telling tales outside of school.'

'Oh, but this isn't like that!' Liv couldn't hold the words back. 'This is… I mean, there's some poor girl out there who—'

Jemima wriggled, gave a loud yawn and then her eyes popped open. A smile wreathed her face when she saw Liv.

Liv's heart expanded to the size of a beach ball. 'Hello, lovely, snuggly-wuggly Jemima. Come and meet Mrs Brown…and Mr Brown,' she added when George came through the back door.

Under the influence of the baby, Mrs Brown's show of stiffness melted. 'Oh, look at you, you wee poppet.'

She was rewarded with a big smile and much waving of arms.

Liv slid a glance at Seb, to find him staring at the baby. His face had softened, making him look younger and less buttoned-up. Her insides turned to mush. She swallowed and glanced back at Mrs Brown, who was playing peekaboo with a delighted Jemima. 'Mrs Brown, would you mind holding Jemima for me while I warm up a bottle? She's due for a feed soon.'

She watched the other woman wrestle with duty and desire—in other words, what she saw as her duty, which was to heat the bottle herself, and her desire, which was to hold Jemima. Liv held her breath.

Holding the baby won out.

Liv heated the bottle.

Seb filled George in on the tale of Jemima.

When Liv returned to the table, Mrs Brown motioned her back to her chair. 'You finish your coffee, lass. I can feed the little one.'

Liv watched and waited. She helped herself

to another scone. Eventually Mrs Brown lifted her head to meet Seb's gaze. 'Over the years two women that I know about have come here to the house claiming that Lord Tyrell fathered their children.'

Seb stiffened. 'Do you remember their names?'

The older woman sighed. 'I have them written down. It might take me some time to search them out. I should have them for you in the morning.'

'Thank you, Brownie.'

'You have to understand that those accounts could be false, so don't go getting your hopes up. They were never taken any further. You don't need me telling you the sort of tricks a certain kind of woman can play when she has a mind to.'

A look passed between Seb and his housekeeper that made Liv's heart thump. She guessed it had something to do with that *unhealthy* relationship he'd mentioned.

She recalled the stone-cold angles of his face when he'd spoken of it and had to repress a shudder. He'd warned her off—it'd been under the guise of sharing a confidence, but she had every intention of heeding that warning. There was no way she was falling for someone so... frozen, someone who'd simply replace her when she flounced off *in a huff.* She didn't know how men could be so cold-blooded when it came to sex, but it appeared they were. One day she'd fall in love again *with a nice man*. Sebastian Tyrell *wasn't* that man.

And yet the shadows in his eyes continued to plague her. She shook her head. She should be concentrating all her efforts on Jemima. Not Seb. Seb could look after himself.

'We need to find her mother.' All eyes turned to her. 'It's the only decent thing to do.'

'Aye.' Mrs Brown nodded. 'Unfortunately, Ms Gilmour, not all mothers are created equal.'

Was she talking about Seb's mother? Liv swallowed, not daring to look at him—even as the memory of haunted eyes taunted her. 'I know, but...' She tilted her chin. 'I'm going to keep an open mind about Jemima's mother until we know the facts.'

'Aye.'

She couldn't stand it any longer. She turned to Seb. 'Are you OK?'

His head went back and his nostrils flared. 'Of course I am. Why wouldn't I be?'

Oh, Seb. 'Because you just found out that you have two potential siblings.'

'Half-siblings,' he corrected.

Did he really think that made any difference?

She turned back to Mrs Brown absurdly close to tears. She needed to keep busy and she suspected Seb did too. 'We were wondering if there might be old letters, diaries...photo albums that we could

scour for possible clues. I know it's a long shot,'
she added when Mrs Brown opened her mouth,
'but we need to start somewhere.'

Mrs Brown glanced at Seb, and Liv had a feeling she'd come to the same conclusion—give Seb
an occupation. She handed Jemima back to Liv.
'If you'd like to follow me…'

They walked through an array of rooms—
rooms that probably had names like the Morning
Room, the Green Sitting Room, and the Breakfast Room—and up the sweeping grand staircase
into a room that led directly off the landing. It was
large and preposterously ornate, and she had to
bite back a gasp of awe. Its perfect dimensions,
high ceilings and the row of tall windows marching down the length of the room and reflecting the
view outside made her ache to set up with paints
and easel. The furniture, though…ugh! She managed not to scowl at it—just. They were all delicate pieces of white and gold nonsense that looked
as if they'd break upon contact. There was only
one substantial piece of furniture in the room, and
that was a leather armchair that sat by the fireplace. Seb's chair, she'd bet.

Mrs Brown went to a long cabinet and pulled
forth a wooden box, several folders and four large
photo albums. She set them on one of the larger
tables. Liv held her breath, but the table bore their
weight without crumpling. 'That's probably as

good a place to start as any,' the housekeeper said before bustling over to start a fire.

It wasn't really cold enough to warrant a fire, but Liv, for one, welcomed its cheer.

She set Jemima's carrier down on an oriental rug—Jemima was busy munching on a teething ring—and seized the box to shove it into Seb's hands. 'Why don't you start with that?'

She didn't want to read personal letters addressed to his family. She collected up the photo albums, glanced around, and then sat cross-legged on the floor beside Jemima.

Seb halted half in his chair. 'You don't have to sit on the floor.'

'I like the floor.' She pointed at the furniture. 'Besides, none of that looks like it's actually made for sitting in. And I don't want to break it.'

He followed the direction of her hand and his nose wrinkled. 'It won't break, but, I agree, it looks far from comfortable.'

It was his house…his furniture. If he didn't like it, why didn't he change it?

He stood. 'You can have my chair.'

'No, no, I'm fine on the floor, I promise. I like it. I can stretch out as I like. Besides, the rug is thick and soft. It's all good.'

He stared at her for a long moment. She resisted the impulse to check her face. 'What?'

'You like to…stretch out?'

Oops. 'I don't *stretch out* in the office, if that's what you're worried about. When I'm at the office I'm all buttoned-up and professional with not a hair out of place.' She stuck out her chin and tried not to glare at him. 'But, as you've no doubt noticed, we're not currently in the office.'

'No.' He subsided back into his chair.

She seized the top album and opened it, effectively bringing their conversation to an end. She didn't want him looking out for her comfort, she didn't want him looking at her, and she didn't want to keep remembering the shadows in his eyes!

She worked her way through the first album. She frowned. Her heart started to thump. She worked her way through the second, the third… and finally the fourth. She closed it with a snap and her hands clenched up so tight her arms started to shake.

'Eliza?'

She leapt up and raced over to one of the windows, dragging big breaths into her lungs. Those albums!

'What's wrong?' He raced across to her. 'What have you found?'

She swung around and the concern on his face pierced her to her marrow. She pointed a shaking finger at the offending albums. 'Where are you?'

Her own family's albums were so different. *So different!*

He blinked. 'What do you mean?'

'Where are you in those photographs?' It was all she could do not to stamp her feet. 'There are pictures of parties and holidays and concerts and yachts and all sorts of amazing things, but you're not in a single one of them!' Because he hadn't been there. Because his own parents had excluded him.

He stilled and then pressed the fingers of one hand to his forehead and rubbed, as if trying to shift a headache. The anger that had whirled through her like a dervish settled into a low burn in her belly. She had to fight the desire to fling her arms about him and hold him tight, to tell him he'd deserved more—so much more.

'There are official photos of my birth, christening…things like that.'

'They're not the pictures I'm interested in.'

He nodded and met her gaze. 'My parents didn't want children.'

That was evident! 'Then why…?'

'It was the one dutiful thing they did do—produce an heir to carry on the family name.'

'Oh, well, let's just pin a medal on them, shall we?'

Her throat thickened. Funny, wasn't it? Here he was, so responsible and conscientious…and yet, producing an heir was the one duty he wasn't interested in fulfilling. She swallowed, hating the reasons that must've led him to that decision. 'So they had you and…what, just abandoned you?' They'd abandoned him as effectively as poor Jemima had been abandoned.

His lips twisted and he shook his head. 'Abandoned me to an army of household staff and a life of privilege. It's not exactly a hard-luck story.' He sent her a small smile. 'And despite everything, I am rather glad to be alive.'

Was he? Then why wasn't he living life…*more*?

She shook that thought off. How could his parents have done it? How could they have treated him so…? A hundred words rallied for selection, but one stood out above the others: coldly. How could they have had so little regard for his feelings? What dreadful people they must be.

He'd deserved so much more than what they'd given him. She wished there were some way it could all be made up to him, but she knew there wasn't. And that seemed like such a tragedy.

Sebastian wasn't quite sure what to make of the expression in her eyes. 'Don't take it so much to heart, Eliza. I don't.' Not any more.

'I'm sorry.' She shook herself and gave a funny little hiccup. 'You deserve so much better than that.'

'Hey…' He bent down until he was on eye level with her. 'Are you crying?' She averted her gaze, but he swept a thumb gently beneath one of her eyes and it came away wet. 'Hey, don't cry. It's OK.'

'No.' She shook her head. 'It really isn't.'

That was when he finally interpreted the expression in her eyes—heartbreak. Heartbreak *for him*! A lump lodged in his throat. He gathered her in and held her close until her head rested against his shoulder and the scent of gardenias and jam rose up all around him. Her free arm slid about his waist and she hugged him back.

Holding her like this felt right in a way that nothing else ever had. He dropped his cheek to her hair and just breathed her in. He wasn't sure for how long they stood like that…or how long they'd have continued—he'd have been content to stay there the rest of the afternoon—but Jemima gave a loud squawk, demanding attention, and, reluctantly, at least on his part, they eased away.

'I'm sorry,' she murmured, moving across to pick up the baby and cuddle her.

'No need to apologise.' She'd cried for him? He couldn't quite believe it. It touched him deep in some centre he'd never known he had. It made his heart beat more firmly. It sent the blood rushing through his veins with renewed vigour. And it made his skin hyper-sensitive.

Desire?

Yes.

And no.

He had a feeling that where this woman was concerned desire would always figure in the equation. But this was something apart from that… something…

Unsettling. But was it good or bad?

His fingers flexed. *It could be dangerous.*

The thought whispered through him. Gooseflesh lifted all of the fine hairs on his arms.

'I was expecting a certain…decorum in the photos, with your family being nobility and whatnot, but I wasn't expecting you to be invisible. I was expecting something…'

'Something?'

'Something *more*. Some show of affection or regard for you. Something of worth!'

Jemima's face crumpled at her nanny's outraged tone and Eliza did her best to hush and comfort her.

Sebastian's stomach churned. 'I can see why you'd be disappointed.'

'Disappointed?'

Air whistled out from between her teeth, telling him she considered that the understatement of the century.

'Better words would be appalled…horrified. I—' She broke off to stalk back to the baby carrier. She rummaged among the blankets and emerged with a disposable nappy. 'Your…your parents should be—' she waved the nappy in the air, evidently searching for a suitable fate '—put in the stocks!'

It was fascinating to see her so riled. Energy crackled from her like static electricity. He glanced at her autumn hair, and then at the way her legs barely seemed to contain her outrage—moving back and forth, feet tapping. He swallowed and a pulse kicked to life at the base of his throat. An answering pulse started low in his groin. He shifted, biting back a groan.

'I wish I could take you home to my parents. They'd make a proper fuss of you like you deserve.'

Warmth flooded through him. Who knew that beneath all that efficiency his PA had such a kind heart?

She stilled. 'I mean… I didn't mean that as…'

He took pity on her. 'I know.'

She glanced around the room. 'I think I hate this house.'

And then she spread out one of Jemima's blankets on the Persian rug and placed the baby on top, changing her nappy with a deftness that made him blink. He stared at those hands, imagined them on his body…

He wrenched his mind back to find her dropping the wet nappy in a plastic bag she'd pulled from her pocket. She rose easily, as if dealing with babies and their paraphernalia were the easiest thing in the world. As if it were second nature to her.

He took the baby blanket and plastic bag from her.

'Eliza.' He reached out and pressed a finger to her lips. Their softness, the caress of her breath against his skin…the way those lips parted the slightest fraction at the pressure of his touch had him clenching up tight.

With a gasp she took a hasty step back, and his hand dropped to his side. 'Yes?'

Her voice came out too breathy and too fast. It was all he could do not to reach for her. He clenched his hands to fists and ordered himself to re-establish normality between them quick smart. 'I…'

He cleared his throat and tried again. 'Don't let my peculiar upbringing poison any of the beauty you find here. Seeing Tyrell Hall through your eyes when we first arrived—through your highly honed artist's eyes,' he teased, his stomach un-clenching a fraction when she smiled back. 'It made me see that's what I've been doing. This house is a masterpiece…set in magnificent sur-roundings. Just because a couple of reprehensible people happened to live here for a while shouldn't blind anyone to the beauty the estate has to offer.'

She stared at him and then gave a nod, her chin coming up. 'You're right.'

She went to say something else but Brownie bustled into the room. 'Ms Gilmour, I thought you might like to see your room...freshen up and take care of the little one.'

'That'd be lovely.'

Not ready to be left alone with his thoughts, Sebastian seized the baby carrier and trailed after them. He smiled when they stopped at the door of the Rose Bedroom. It was the loveliest of the guest bedrooms.

'Oh!'

Eliza's eyes went wide when they entered. Very carefully she set the baby on the bed to turn on the spot and take in her room. 'I'm going to feel like royalty sleeping in here.'

The room had a four-poster bed with a smoky-pink silken canopy, the hangings embroidered with blue, white and yellow roses. The same accents were picked up in the curtains at the two windows. The walls were painted the palest of pinks and a rug of pink and white made a warm contrast to the dark floorboards. Her windows looked north over fields to woodland.

'It's absolutely and utterly divine! But—' She swung around. 'Mrs Brown, I'm just the nanny. Surely I—'

'Nonsense! This room rarely gets used. It'll be nice to have someone in here enjoying it for a few days.'

That was when Sebastian spotted the cot in the corner. He pointed to it. 'There's been a mistake. The cot needs to go into the room next door. I'm sharing night-time baby duties with Ms Gilmour.' He glanced at Eliza. 'My bedroom is two doors down, which will work out perfectly.'

Eliza planted her hands on her hips, unintentionally directing his attention to how those hips flared gently in the soft woollen trousers she wore. The collar about his throat tightened. His hands itched to trace her outline from neck to waist…and further. His fingers craved to sink into the softness of the flesh of her backside and to—'

'No!'

His attention snapped back. The colour high on her cheeks betrayed her awareness of his scrutiny. He swallowed. 'I beg your pardon?'

'I said *no*.'

She was saying no to…?

'You're paying me to be Jemima's nanny, and that's exactly what I mean to be.'

The thread that held him tight released him when he realised she was referring to her role as nanny. He pulled in a breath and tried not to look too relieved.

'It was an altogether different thing when I was thrust into the role with no warning and then had three sleepless nights. But I'm better rested now.'

But not fully rested.

She lifted Jemima back into her arms. 'I've kept this little monkey awake for a greater part of the morning. And I mean to do the same for the rest of the afternoon.'

He shuffled his feet. 'But—'

'And now we have those talking books I expect things will start to fall into place.'

He tried to think of an argument to convince her to let him help.

'You'll have oodles of time to play with her to-morrow.' She shot Brownie a grin. 'This little miss has him wrapped firmly around her little finger.'

'Well, she's such a sweet thing.' Brownie cast an undeniably hopeful glance at Eliza. 'If you need any assistance at all, Ms Gilmour, I'd only be too happy to help out.'

'Oh, that's kind of you.'

'I took the liberty of unpacking the baby bag and I've made up a couple of fresh bottles. So if you'd like me to take her back down to the kitchen…'

He saw the exact moment Liv registered Brownie's yearning to fuss over the baby—if only for half an hour. She glanced at her watch. 'Are you sure you wouldn't mind? I'd kill for a shower.'

Brownie promptly took Jemima from her arms. 'It's no problem whatsoever. Why don't you have a nice long soak in the tub instead? Me and the little one here will have a fine old time getting to know one another.'

'A bath? Ooh, you're an angel, Mrs Brown.'

'You take your time, Ms Gilmour. Master Sebastian, show Ms Gilmour where to find the bathroom and then come down to the kitchen so I can tell you about all the local happenings.'

'I've been away less than a fortnight; I—' He broke off with a nod and a half-grin at the glare she sent him. 'Yes, ma'am.'

'I'm timing you,' she shot at him as she stalked from the room.

'That was a nice thing to do,' he said once Brownie was out of earshot.

'It was nice of her to offer. Besides, she's lovely.'

'Still, you could've kept Jemima all to yourself and nobody would've blamed you. It's kind of you to share.'

She frowned. 'Seb?'

'What?' He had to resist the urge to move closer to her. Moving closer wouldn't be wise.

Her frown deepened, countered by the worry in her eyes. 'I know we both feel a great deal of responsibility towards Jemima, but you can't forget that she doesn't belong to us.'

A scowl built through him. He rolled his shoulder. 'I know that.'

'Do you?' Her eyes refused to release his. 'If we do this right we'll reunite Jemima with her mother. After that it's possible we'll never see her again.'

An unexpected pain slipped in between his ribs.

She tapped a fist against her mouth. 'I… I just want you to be prepared.'

Never see that little baby again? Never know if she was safe and happy? Everything inside of him rebelled at the thought. 'How is it possible to prepare for that?' It took all his strength not to shout the words.

She sucked her bottom lip into her mouth and he sensed the same turmoil roiling through her. 'By believing it's what's best for Jemima.'

He pulled in a breath and nodded, tried to regulate his breathing. 'Yes.'

But what if Jemima's mother was like his own?

She moved towards the door, but paused beside him. She touched his shoulder. 'It's just… I'd hate to see you get hurt.'

The warmth of her hand did strange things to his insides. She pulled her fingers back as if suddenly burned and sent him an over-bright smile. 'Now, show me where the bathroom is. A long, hot soak is exactly what the doctor ordered.'

He led the way and refused to fantasise for a single moment on what her naked body would look like sliding into a tub of steaming water.

CHAPTER SIX

LIV DIDN'T SEE Seb at breakfast the next morning. Last night they'd sat up going through the documents Mrs Brown had dug out, but they were left none the wiser. The documents and letters hadn't divulged any deep and dark secrets. She glanced across the rim of her coffee mug. Had the housekeeper provided Seb with those names this morning? Was he holed up somewhere brooding...and haunted?

She set her mug down. He might simply want some solitude from his too-bossy, too-chatty office manager. The thought made her wince.

When Mrs Brown didn't give her any message from him, she refused to ask his whereabouts. It wasn't as if she didn't have plenty to do looking after Jemima. And she really ought to get started on that detailed outline on events for Liz.

She didn't need to send it yet. Liz didn't need the worry. But her sister would need to know more than just the basics before she returned.

Liz hadn't phoned last night as she'd promised either. Liv didn't know whether to be relieved or worried. She'd sent Liz an email asking her how things were going...and when she thought she'd be coming home.

She was still waiting for a reply.

'What are your plans for the day, Ms Gilmour?'

Liv snapped herself back into the present. 'I'm going to take this little one,' she jigged Jemima who was currently ensconced on her knee, 'out in her pram for her daily dose of sunshine.' She took a big sip of coffee. The sooner she was out in the day the better. She felt in serious need of sunshine herself.

'You should stroll up to the artists' co-operative.'

Her ears pricked up. 'Artists' co-op?'

'Aye. Master Sebastian had the barn and a few of the other outbuildings converted into studios with spaces for local artists to sell their wares. He wanted to showcase local talent.'

She stared at Mrs Brown, her mug halted half-way to her mouth. 'Really?'

The housekeeper chuckled. 'You look surprised.'

'I...' She blinked and lowered her mug. 'I had no idea he was interested in art.'

'Ah, well, he's not. Not personally. But a large portion of the estate had to be sold off to cover the debts that had accrued.'

Debts incurred by his profligate parents, no doubt.

'A great chunk of farming land had to go—land leased to local farmers.' The older woman shook her head. 'It was a terrible business. A lot of good folk lost their livelihoods.'

Because of the selfishness of two negligent, un-principled snobs? Her hands clenched and she had to concentrate on not jiggling Jemima right off her knee.

'So Master Sebastian, in an effort to help rein-vigorate the local community, had the outbuildings converted and offered the spaces to local artists and craftspeople.'

He was trying to make amends for his parents' lavish spending. He was trying to make a differ-ence. A good difference. He was a good man.

'Aye, that he is.'

She blinked and realised she'd said the words out loud.

'The public are invited to drop in during busi-ness hours to see the artists at work and to buy what they've made. You won't be disturbing any-one if you go up there. They're a lovely bunch, al-ways up for a natter.'

It was obvious that Mrs Brown was proud of the initiative and Liv didn't need any further con-vincing. She drained her mug and stood. 'It sounds perfect.'

Ten minutes later Liv was pushing Jemima's pram along the neat gravel path that led towards the art-ists' co-op. The collection of buildings was located to the north-east of the hall, and as she drew closer she saw that the complex had its own separate entrance from the road and its own small car park, which was already a third full.

She glanced down at Jemima, busily chewing on her teddy bear. 'This could be fun, Jemmy Jemima Jo-Jo.'

Jemima gurgled her delight and appreciation at Liv's sing-song silliness.

She'd not had a good dose of arts and crafts in an age. She might not paint herself any more, but it didn't stop her from admiring the work of others. She regularly frequented the galleries and exhibitions of London to get her fill, by proxy, of creativity, artistic endeavour and beauty. It replenished her in a way that nothing else could.

And as always happened, the closer she drew to the gallery—or in this instance, the artists' co-op—the lighter she became, as if just being near art freed something inside of her. All her worries temporarily lifted from her shoulders. She glanced up at the sky and smiled. It was almost impossible to cling to her anxiety in the face of such beautiful weather in a rural idyll like this, especially with the promise of such a treat in front of her.

The proverbial cherry on the cake, though, was that she'd been seen coming from 'the Big House'. Once it was established that she and Jemima were friends of Mr Sebastian's, they were welcomed with unstinting warmth that spoke volumes of the high regard Seb was held in by the members of the community here.

The blacksmith and his apprentice snaffled her first to tour their forge in a separate building set slightly apart from the others. They showed her the beautiful cast-iron candlesticks and bookends they made and had proven such a hit with the general public. 'We're starting to take orders via our website,' they told her proudly.

She could've stayed there for hours except that the potters bore her off to the main barn building. There she marvelled at decorative glazed tiles and plates, and drooled over the jugs, vases and beer steins. 'We have a kiln and pottery wheels in a part of the old coach house. It's ideal.' She promised to come back if she had time later in the week and try her hand on the pottery wheel.

Between them, the weavers and leather workers explained how they paid a nominal rent for their spaces, but that the money wasn't ploughed back into the estate. Instead it was used to maintain the complex and make any improvements that the members voted on—like the café that was currently under discussion. Liv asked them to put away a woollen shawl and one of the leather-tooled journal covers for her and she'd come back tomorrow with the money. She added a tie-dyed silk scarf in the most amazing colours to her growing list of purchases. 'It'll match your hair,' the dyer laughed.

She moved along to the next studio—a jewellery maker. One glimpse at the wares and Liv came to the crushing conclusion that her own attempts were embarrassingly amateur.

Oh, well. She only did it for fun.

Finally—with the leather worker's assistance with the pram—she ascended to the mezzanine level to view the paintings and sketches that the three local artists were working on, and the finished artworks they had for sale. Her chest burned when she glanced at an easel complete with a readied canvas just waiting for an artist to start work. But she had no time to brood as Naomi, Helen and Dirk—the artists—introduced themselves.

They fell into an immediate and rapt conversation. She quizzed Naomi on her use of light and shade, fascinated with the effects she'd created among sun-dappled leaves and mist-shrouded tree trunks in her woodland collection of paintings. She and Dirk then became engrossed in a discussion about structure and perspective. With Helen it was modernism and her bold choice of colours that they analysed. It left her feeling alternatively breathless and invigorated. She hadn't felt this alive in...*years*!

'C'mon, then.' Helen held out a sketchpad with a grin.

Liv crashed back to reality. 'I...' She swallowed. 'What do you mean?'

'Don't give us that,' Dirk chided. 'It's obvious you're an artist too. You've an artist's eye, not to mention an artist's vocabulary.'

'I… I just love art.' At their raised eyebrows, she gave up. 'I don't paint any more.' Her heart thumped with bruising power as she said the words.

The three artists exchanged glances. Helen swung back. 'You don't have to paint.' And then she frogmarched Liv to a stool and set the sketch-pad on an easel in front of her.

'Oh, but—'

'Sketch,' she ordered her.

She swallowed. 'I don't do that any more either.'

'Artist's block,' Naomi diagnosed. And at her words all three of them sprang into action. Naomi flipped the sketchpad open, while Helen selected a pencil and pushed it into Liv's hand, neither woman giving her the chance to dither over the choice.

Dirk wheeled the baby closer. 'Sketch the baby,' he instructed. 'She's asleep, so it'll be a doddle.'

She glared at him. 'A doddle? Babies aren't a doddle, they're—'

'Don't think, draw,' he ordered.

With a sigh, she gave in and started a sketch. As soon as they saw her pitiable efforts they'd retreat and leave her in peace. She started but soon made a mistake. Naomi turned the page of the sketchpad, not giving her any time to dwell on her mistake. 'Start again.'

It happened twice more—stupid mistakes that in her heyday she'd have never made—but Naomi refused to allow her to dwell on the errors, just kept urging her forward.

The feel of the pencil in her hand was as familiar as the rise and fall of her own breath. And as she stared down at Jemima, remembering her in all her moods, the pencil started to fly across the page. She sketched and she shaded and then she turned the page, seized a stick of charcoal and did it all again in a bolder style.

And then she stopped to survey her handiwork. She stared at it and her throat closed over. She couldn't have uttered a word if her life depended on it.

This sketch...it was a halfway decent effort. Better than anything she'd attempted in the last four years.

Her heart starting to beat hard. Actually, it was better than all right. It was...*good*.

She gripped her hands together so hard they started to ache. She was too afraid to hope, too afraid to let the wild exhilaration spinning through her free. But... Had her gift come back?

How?

Was it even possible?

Her mind spun.

The three other artists passed the pad from one to the other silently. 'This isn't just good,' Helen finally said, her voice full of awe. 'This… You have an amazing talent.'

She stared at them, lifted her hands and let them drop, absurdly close to tears. 'I thought I'd lost it.'

'You don't just *lose* a gift like this,' Dirk told her.

When had it come back? How? 'If you three hadn't bullied me I might've gone the rest of my life not realising I could still do this.' And the thought now seemed too awful to consider.

'That wouldn't have happened. You'd have picked up a pencil again. You'd have not been able to help yourself. How long since…?'

'Four years.'

The three artists stared at her in varying shades of shock and horror. 'Four years,' Dirk finally said. 'Where were your artist friends? Why weren't they pushing and nagging you?'

'I…' She'd pushed them all away, cut herself off from them, too ashamed to face them.

'Never mind that now,' Naomi said with a smile. 'What's your preferred medium—oils or water-colours?'

'Oils,' she whispered.

Naomi nodded at the sketchpad. 'Would you like to give that a whirl on canvas?'

A smile rose through her. 'Yes, please.'

* * *

Sebastian came to a halt, his foot resting on the last riser up to the mezzanine level in the refurbished barn. Brownie had sent him across to the co-op in search of Eliza…and it seemed his search had come to an end.

She stood in front of a canvas *painting*, and his heart started to thump. She somehow managed to look completely alien and totally familiar, both at the same time. Yet…he'd never seen her like this before—totally immersed in the project in front of her, her brow crinkled with a kind of intense concentration that was interspersed with bursts of fiery movement.

What on earth had happened to his sensible office manager? How could he have got this woman so wrong? For a moment he couldn't move. All he could do was stare.

She looked… Powerful.

Energy coursed through her—setting her lips with purpose, curling her fingers about the brush and rag she held as if they were part of her. Energy crackled all around her, as if she had her own electrical force field.

A beat started up at the centre of him—a pulse that had the same intensity, the same sense of purpose. He didn't know what it meant or what it signified. He only knew that for long, deep moments he couldn't move, couldn't look away, couldn't even breathe, as he felt the world shifting and himself falling through space...all while his feet remained planted firmly on the floor.

A glance about the room told him he wasn't the only one mesmerised. A crowd stood around in an expectant hush—the three artists and several potential customers. The only one not the least concerned was Jemima, who nestled in Dirk's arms—he had three little ones at home—intently sucking on her bottle.

Naomi glanced across at him. Putting a finger to her lips, she beckoned him over. As a child he'd learned to walk silently to avoid his parents' notice. He brought those skills into play now as he moved to Naomi's side several feet behind the absorbed artist at work, where he'd get a partial view of the painting in progress.

What he saw made the pulse in his throat pound while his lips parted to drag in more air. He didn't need to be fluent in art appreciation to realise that what he saw on that canvas wasn't just good—it was amazing. He raised an eyebrow at Naomi, who shook her head and shrugged.

Eliza had all but completed a painting of a sleeping Jemima, but the bold strokes and the texture of the paint didn't just capture the innocence and peace of the sleeping baby—it also captured Jemima's mischievousness, her laughter...but something darker was hinted at too in the colours bleeding out at the edges of the canvas. Those colours suggested turmoil…mourned a paradise lost. He couldn't capture or explain all of the emotions that flashed back and forth through him—he only knew that Eliza's painting seized him in a fast grip and then shook him like a rag doll.

Jemima finished her bottle and Sebastian gave up silent thanks that Eliza refused to sally forth without a ready-made bottle to spare…just in case. Dirk lifted the baby to his shoulder to burp her, but Jemima saw Sebastian and gave a squeal of delight, making everyone jump.

Eliza didn't jump, but it did pull her from whatever world she'd inhabited. She turned slowly as if emerging from a dream. Those golden eyes rested on him for a moment before surveying the rest of the room. She had a smudge of pink and white paint on her cheek, and her right hand was covered in the stuff. He watched as astonishment and then consternation passed across her face, before she swung back to her painting and stilled.

All of them held their breath as she surveyed her artwork.

She set the brush and rag down to a nearby workbench and folded her arms. She unfolded them a moment later to plant her hands on her hips. She moved from one side of the painting to the other—bent at the waist to examine a detail here and there, moved back to study it from a distance.

Eventually she turned to face the small crowd behind her and lifted her hands before letting them drop back to her sides. 'It's good.'

'Good?' Naomi sprang forward. 'It's amazing!'

And then Sebastian found himself holding the baby while the other two artists rushed to join Naomi, the four artists hugging each other and talking at once, and all Sebastian could do was watch and wish he could be a part of it.

Which was crazy. He shifted and jiggled Jemima.

'I want to buy it!' One of the customers leapt forward, pulling his wallet from his back pocket. 'How much?'

Every muscle he possessed stiffened. 'It's not for sale!'

The customer bristled. 'I offered first and I'm not going to let you undercut me. Let the woman speak for herself. Who do you think you are anyway?'

Helen pointed back the way Sebastian had come. 'He's Lord Tyrell's son…he owns this place.'

'Oh.' Crestfallen, the customer shoved his wallet back into his pocket.

Eliza met Sebastian's eyes. 'It *isn't* for sale.' And he realised that she was talking to him, telling him he couldn't have it either.

He opened his mouth to protest. He wanted that painting with every fibre of his being. But the customer—who evidently wanted it as much as Sebastian…and, who knew, maybe they had identical expressions on their faces?—leapt forward with a second wind. 'I'll pay good money.' And then he named a sum that made Sebastian's eyes water.

Eliza shook her head. 'I'm sorry this particular painting isn't for sale. But if you come back next week, who knows what you might find?' she said with a smile to soften her refusal.

Dimly he was aware of her making arrangements for the painting with the other artists and then she was at his side, taking Jemima from his arms and settling her back in her pram.

'I'm starving! It must be time for lunch.'

He kicked himself out of his stupor. 'Brownie sent me to find you. She said you'd been gone for hours.'

She flicked a glance at her watch and her eyes widened. 'She's right. Heavens! Come on.'

He helped her manoeuvre the pram back to the ground floor, noted the friendly waves she exchanged with everyone, before turning in the direction of the hall. They were halfway along the gravel path and his pulse still hadn't returned to its right rhythm, the ground beneath his feet still hadn't stopped shifting. 'Are you going to explain that?' he finally burst out.

She halted to stare up at him. It was only then

that he realised her appearance of calm was a sham. Behind the gold of her eyes everything raced and boiled.

'I mean I thought you were a super-cool and efficient PA.'

The gold in her eyes dimmed a fraction.

'But then you transformed into… Mother Earth.'

'Oh, that's hardly an apt description.'

'And now…now you're *an artist*?'

Those eyes were abruptly removed from his. 'Not…not an artist, but… I used to like to paint. A lot.'

'Of course you're an artist. I just witnessed it with my own eyes!'

Her shoulders inched up towards her ears. 'Well, as I said, I used to like to paint, but… I stopped for a while and…and I thought… I thought I'd lost it.'

How could you lose…*that*?

'But it appears I haven't.'

In an instant her shoulders unhitched and it was as if she couldn't keep her smile in for another moment, it blazed out full of life and hope, and Sebastian found his heart beating hard and fast. For the briefest of moments she tossed her head back to beam at the sky and as he stared at the long, lean line of her throat something pierced into him, making him hungry for…for something that was more than sex. Something he couldn't name.

'Thank you for bringing me here, Seb.' She

reached forward to seize his hand. 'You've no idea what it means to me.'

'I'll accept the painting as payment.' He had no idea he'd meant to say that until the words shot out of his mouth, but that painting had reached out and grabbed him by the heart, much as Jemima had.

She dropped his hand and he immediately wished the words unsaid. Her hair fanned out about her face as she shook her head. 'I'm sorry, but that painting is mine. You've no idea how hard-won it was.' Clouds chased themselves across her face. 'That painting will make sure I *never* forget.'

She smiled so suddenly it momentarily blinded him and he wondered if his heart would ever return to normal again.

'But I'm awfully chuffed you like it so much. I'll paint you something else,' she promised.

An ache started up deep down inside him. 'You say you thought you'd lost it?'

She nodded and started pushing the pram again.

'What did you mean? Will you explain it to me?'

She bit her lip. 'Oh, I'm not sure there's much to explain. I…'

He didn't buy that for a single moment. 'Over lunch.'

Brownie seated them out in the courtyard in the sun and served them steaming bowls of vegetable and barley soup, crusty bread and a jug of beer before whisking Jemima back into the kitchen with her.

Liv grinned at the food. 'This doesn't exactly look like lord-of-the-manor fare.'

'Brownie knows what I like.' He poured her a glass of beer, and then paused. 'If you'd prefer something else—'

'No, no!' She sampled the soup and closed her eyes in appreciation. 'This is perfect.'

He didn't want to waste time on preliminaries. 'So...what did you mean earlier?'

She didn't pretend to misunderstand him but nor did she allay his curiosity. 'You first.'

She had to be joking! Seeing her paint had shifted something inside of him, changed him in a fundamental way he didn't want to examine too closely. And it had changed her too. He sensed it. And yet she wanted to talk about—

'Did you get those names from Mrs Brown?'

And just like that the world slammed back into place—the way it had been before he'd seen her paint. She was right. They were here to find Jemima's mother. Anything else was of little importance, and yet he continued to let himself get distracted.

He let *her* distract him.

His heart pounded with a sick realisation. He'd been wrong about Eliza Gilmour. She wasn't some cool and efficient, buttoned-up office manager, no matter how much she might assume that façade at work. It didn't mean she couldn't be trusted, but it reminded him of all the ways he'd misjudged Rhoda, of how he'd let his desire for family and belonging blind him.

He wasn't making that same mistake again.

He had to be careful. Lust and desire were evolving into a dangerous fascination he couldn't afford to entertain. He had to resist it. He set his spine. He *would* resist it. For God's sake, Eliza was an employee. He *did not* take advantage of his staff. He *was not* his father.

'Seb?'

He pulled in a breath. 'Soup good?'

'Delicious.'

They sipped their soup, eyeing each other over their bowls with watchful caution. He reached for the bread, cutting off a wedge and slathering it in butter. 'Brownie provided me with the promised names first thing this morning. An internet search hasn't kicked up any additional clues so I've given the names to Jack, my PI.'

She stared at him but he had no idea what was going on behind the golden amber of her eyes. He recalled the way she'd cried the previous afternoon and had to swallow.

'So...you might have two siblings.'

His mouth dried. 'It appears a possibility.'

'Do you, um...want to know them?'

Once he'd ached for family, but now... 'I don't know.'

'It must be a lot to take in.'

He didn't want to talk about it. 'I just want to find Jemima's mother. That's all I'm prepared to focus on at the moment. We now have two potential candidates, which means we're closer to the truth than we were yesterday.'

She abandoned her spoon to slump in her seat. 'These are only the women Mrs Brown knows about, the ones who've come forward. There could be others.'

Countless others.

She grimaced. 'Another thought occurred to me while I was up at the co-op.'

She picked up her spoon again, ran it back and forth through her soup, not meeting his eye. He set his bread down. 'What is it?'

She pulled in a breath. 'Mrs Brown explained to me earlier that to save the estate you had to sell off a large portion of land.'

He promptly lost his appetite. 'I sold hundreds of acres of farmland. To a conglomerate.' He'd needed to find a large sum fast.

'I understand that created hardship for...for some of the farmers who'd been leasing the land from you.'

'Yes.' The single word coated his tongue in bitterness.

'Oh, Seb, it's not your fault.' She reached across the table towards him, but stopped short of touching him. 'You saved what you could.'

It wasn't how it felt. He should've found a way to curtail his father's spending years ago.

'Is it possible that Jemima could belong to one of them?'

He stared at her. The thought had never occurred to him. Had he made some young mother homeless? He shot to his feet and made for the house.

'Where are you going?' she called after him.

'To ring Jack.'

CHAPTER SEVEN

LIV WAITED, BUT SEB didn't come back to finish his barely touched lunch. Famished, she ate her soup and a good portion of the bread. Losing herself to a painting always made her hungry. She contemplated the events of the morning, trying to make sense of them, swinging between euphoria one moment and fear the next.

What if it was a one-off and the next time she picked up a paintbrush she froze again?

What if it wasn't and what if she didn't?

Had her gift been there all this time, hiding from her, just waiting for her to put in the effort to unearth it?

Why hadn't she kept trying? Why hadn't she proven herself to her muse sooner?

She swallowed. Why had she let shame and guilt conquer her so completely?

"'The bad stuff is easier to believe,'" she murmured, quoting a line from one of her favourite movies. It was easier to believe the worst of oneself rather than the best.

And still Seb didn't come back.

She glanced around the walled garden—the kitchen garden rather than the more formal gardens on the other side of the warm grey stone.

The staked tomatoes and runner beans provided a flourishing backdrop for feathery carrot plants and other vegetables she couldn't identify. Heads of lettuce gleamed in the sun and lemon balm and thyme scented the air from nearby pots. Everything looked lush and vigorous. *She* felt lush and vigorous. She felt full rather than empty.

She glanced over her shoulder. Why hadn't Seb come back?

She frowned, going over their lunchtime conversation—what little there'd been of it. Something had changed in him and it took a while for her to pinpoint the exact moment it had happened. It wasn't when she'd started quizzing him about selling the farmland as she'd first thought. It was when she'd told him he had to go first—to bring her up to date on Jemima's situation.

'Oh!' She stiffened. Had he thought she'd been unwilling to confide in him?

It wasn't that at all! But she'd needed to remind herself what they were doing here, what their priority was—Jemima. She'd been playing for time. She'd love to confide in him, but… How on earth could she and Liz maintain their charade if she did?

But she hadn't meant him to feel excluded, or think she thought him an unworthy confidant.

The bad stuff is easier to believe.

She glanced up at the house. He'd grown up with

those vile parents who must've made him feel excluded and unwanted every single day of his childhood. He'd been honestly interested in what had happened to her this morning. Mystified too, and curious, but interested in a way a friend would be interested—perhaps even a little invested as this was his home and he'd been the one to bring her here. He'd sensed it was a big thing, a turning point, a personal miracle. And so much else here at Tyrell Hall obviously had hateful associations. Rather than sharing her good fortune with him, her excitement and gratitude, she'd dragged him back to ugly realities.

'Oh!' She shot to her feet. She hadn't meant to be mean-spirited! No wonder he hadn't come back.

She raced their two bowls back into the kitchen.

'Don't you wake her,' Mrs Brown ordered when she peered into the pram. 'She's only just gone off.'

Liv picked up the empty tray sitting on the table. 'You have yourself a deal as long as you let me clear away the rest of the lunch things.' When she returned with a laden tray, she said, 'Do you know where Seb went?'

Mrs Brown pointed upstairs. 'I think you'll find him in the drawing room.'

With a swift smile she headed upstairs.

Seb stood by one of the tall windows, staring out at the park, his tall frame silhouetted in all its lean, hard glory. A pulse in her throat kicked to life. She had to swallow before she could speak. 'Seb?'

He swung around. 'Yes?'

The word was clipped out, all the lines about his mouth tight and firm and yet that couldn't hide the natural sensuality of those lips. Not completely.

She moistened her lips and stared at that mouth. She couldn't help wondering—fantasising—how would it feel on hers? How—?

She dragged her gaze back to the fire, her heart pounding. The fire was totally unnecessary in this weather, but she had to admit that it was pleasant. It was the fire flaring to powerful life inside her that was both unnecessary and unpleasant.

No, not unpleasant so much as inconvenient.

'You didn't come back to finish your lunch.'

He waved a hand towards his laptop, open on a nearby coffee table—one of those ridiculous pieces of frivolous nonsense. 'There were several very unhappy people when I sold off that farming land. I kept a record.' His face didn't change by the movement of a single muscle and yet she could sense the tension coiling through him. 'Unfortunately, when you're in a position like mine, you do receive the occasionally threatening and, or, unpleasant letter or email.'

She could imagine. And delving into these particular ones had forced the lid on unpleasant memories.

'I've sent the information to Jack, but…' He shook his head, a frown burrowing into his brow. 'I know it's a legitimate lead, but I can't help feeling we'll have no joy from that area.'

Good. She glanced down at her hands then back up at him. 'Remember my plan to gossip with the estate workers and anyone else I thought might be of use?'

His head swung up. 'Yes.'

'I hadn't been up at the co-op for two minutes before I realised how totally fruitless that would be. You're held in the very highest of regard there.'

He waved that off as if it was of no concern. 'It doesn't change the fact that selling off the farmland left people unemployed. I should've found a different way to deal with it! It's my fault those—'

'Rubbish! You're not the spendthrift here. Whose debts were they? Your parents'? If anyone's to blame, they are. Holding yourself responsible is crazy, Seb. I imagine you were lucky to save what you did.'

But she could tell her words barely touched him. She moved across and shook his arm. 'You've nothing to beat yourself up for. What you've done with the co-op is amazing. Why can't you focus on that?'

He raised a mocking eyebrow, detaching himself from her grip. 'If you tell me I take my responsibilities too seriously, I'll tell you that you sound like my father.'

She took a step back from him.

'And if you claim I take my sense of duty too far, I'll tell you that you sound like my mother.'

She took another step back and nodded, swallowed back the lump that wanted to lodge in her throat. 'Right. Well. I know you must be busy so...'

She turned to leave.

'No! *Stop!* I'm sorry.'

She turned back to find him dragging a hand down his face. He looked so momentarily haggard that her heart went out to him.

'That wasn't fair of me. I...' He lifted a sheaf of paper he'd dropped to the window seat and rustled it in her direction, his lips twisting. 'I've just been rereading the last correspondence between my father and myself. I thought there might be some clue in it that I'd missed.'

She took in the expression on his face, the shadows in his eyes, and in that moment she hated his parents.

'Being confronted with one's shortcomings is far from edifying. Let's see...' He glanced down at the page. 'Now, it's after the piece about the Cresley-Throckmortons being *"frightful prigs"*. Ah, yes, here we go. Apparently I'm a *"dreadfully dull dog who wouldn't know how to have fun if it jumped up and bit me on the nose..."* I have *"a lamentable lack of charm..."* and I'm apparently *"the death of any party"*—which, they believe, is the worst insult that could be levelled at anyone.' He glanced back down at the letter and shrugged. 'I could *"cast a pall over Christmas and they're so very pleased never to have to clap eyes on me again."'* He folded the letter and pushed it back into its envelope. 'It's put me out of...temper.'

She stared at him in growing horror. 'But that's...it's nothing but mean-spirited spite! Because you bailed them from financial ruin and then refused to continue financing their high living.'

'It is indeed.'

But it seemed their attitude still had the power to hurt him.

'And it's no excuse for my shortness to you just now. You didn't deserve it. I apologise.'

'Apology accepted.' She moistened suddenly dry lips. After three beats she said, 'They're wrong, you know.'

Both of his eyebrows shot up towards his hairline. 'But, my dear, the Cresley-Throckmortons *are* frightful prigs.'

She choked back a sudden and entirely inappropriate laugh. 'You know what I mean.'

He sobered, with a shrug. 'It's also true I don't like parties.' He strode across to the fireplace. 'I've no talent for them. They bore me silly.'

She rolled her eyes. 'That just means you haven't been to the right kind of party.'

He stirred the fire with the poker and sparks shot up the chimney.

She stared at him. She planted her hands on her hips. 'It's possible to be honourable, responsible *and* fun, you know? And you are.' Or, at least, she was pretty certain he could be.

'Thank you for the vote of confidence.' His lips lifted but his smile held no real warmth and she could see that he didn't believe her.

Damn and blast and damn!

He glanced up, paralysing her to the spot with those piercing grey eyes. 'Was there something you wanted to talk to me about? Is that why you came looking for me?'

Her first instinct was to deny it, to give him some space, but the words took too long in coming.

He straightened. 'There was.'

'It's nothing that can't keep.'

'And yet there's no time like the present.'

Being the sole focus of those intense grey eyes did seriously unsettling things to her insides. She swallowed and tried to appear unaffected. 'It's just that we didn't finish our lunchtime conversation and I didn't want you thinking I was trying to put you off or deflecting you from asking about what happened this morning at the co-op...with the painting and stuff,' she added in a rush.

He seemed to wrestle with himself for a moment and suddenly she felt like a prize idiot. It could be that he hadn't pursued the topic because he simply wasn't all that interested, and now here she was making a big thing about it and—

'I didn't want to pry into out-of-bounds territory.'

Her heart started to thump. It should be out of bounds.

'But I'd love to know what happened this morning. It seemed…momentous.'

Oh, but he has such awful parents.

She swallowed and then lifted her chin. 'It was. It's hard to describe.'

She couldn't just keep standing here when he stared at her like that—with such intensity. It was too… She just couldn't do it! 'Does Tyrell Hall have one of those wonderfully long galleries lined with portraits of ancestors that one sees in period films?'

'Follow me.'

He took her to a wing at the other end of the house. They passed dim rooms where dustcovers enveloped the furniture. They went up a flight of stairs and she sensed that she stood at one end of a long space, but it wasn't until Seb went along and opened the shutters at the multitude of tall windows that the gallery's glory came to life.

'Oh, my,' she murmured as she moved further into the gallery and glanced up at the first couple of portraits. 'This is splendid.' She pointed along the wall. 'I recognise some of these painters.'

'Would you like a potted history of the Tyrell family?'

She smiled. 'I would, but not today.' She didn't need him to treat her like a child and create an atmosphere where she'd feel comfortable confiding in him. He looked after enough people. He didn't need to look after her too.

She needed to be careful. She needed to keep these details as general as possible. Nothing she told him could conflict with Liz's CV. She pulled in a breath and pointed at the painting above them. 'I can't remember a time when I haven't loved to paint and draw.'

The truth was she'd attended a prestigious art college in London. Big things had been expected of her. Dropping out in her second year hadn't been one of them. Her parents had paid a great deal of money to make sure she'd had a chance to follow her dream. Money they could've spent on Liz's education. Money they could've spent on themselves!

They moved along to the next portrait. She stared at the painting, not at him. 'After I finished secondary school I took some art classes…night classes.' That wasn't a complete lie. Some of her classes had been scheduled in the evening.

'You have an exceptional talent. You should've gone to art school.'

She tried not to wince. 'I wanted job security. And being an artist is not a proper job.' *Liar.*

'So, you took some art classes…?'

She moistened her lips. Now came the difficult part.

'What happened?'

'I loved them.'

'But?' he prompted when she faltered.

She'd wanted to confide in him because she wanted him to know that she saw him as someone worth confiding in, that she valued him, because she wanted him to feel good about himself. Oh, but her confession was so shameful!

He was no longer pretending to gaze at the portraits. He was staring at her, and she could no longer ignore his silent demand that she meet his gaze. The very air about her seemed to throb. 'But I had a torrid affair with my teacher.'

He stilled. 'How old were you?'

She swallowed. 'Nineteen.'

His nostrils flared and his eyes grew hard and flinty. 'How old was this teacher?'

She nodded. 'He was more than twice my age, but very good-looking and suave.' She pulled in a breath and sent him an apologetic smile. 'He seemed so…sophisticated. I can see now how he took advantage of my relative inexperience, but at the time I was smitten.'

He reached out and seized her shoulders. 'You've

nothing to feel guilty about. Do you understand me? There are men out there that prey on young women and—'

He released her to pace to the window. He stalked back, his hands clenched. 'What was his name? He should be exposed…punished…horsewhipped.'

At that moment he looked more than capable of doing exactly that. The momentary heat from his hands continued to burn through her, and the thought of him exacting revenge on her behalf had her tingling all over. She moistened her lips, suddenly thirsty for a taste him.

She had to stop thinking of him like this!

As if aware of the direction of her wayward thoughts, he stilled and then his gaze lowered to her lips. They darkened with a barely disguised hunger, and wind roared in her ears. She had to fight the urge to run her tongue over her lips again, to taunt him into action. At the last moment she wrenched herself away and moved to stare unseeingly out of the window.

It was a moment before he spoke again. 'Do you still care for him?'

She swung around at that. 'No!'

'But he hurt you.'

She couldn't deny it. She tried to control the pounding of her heart, tried to keep the conversation on track. 'At the time I was convinced he'd broken my heart and that I'd never recover.' She twisted her hands together, fighting the shame that wanted to devour her. 'But he did something far worse than break off our affair. He poked fun at my paintings, undermined my confidence, told me I'd never amount to...to anything.' And she'd been stupid enough to believe him. 'Why would he do that?' She still didn't understand it.

She watched in fascination as his hands clenched into fists. 'He sounds as small-minded and contemptible as my parents. I suspect he was jealous of your work, probably felt like a failure when he compared it to yours.'

'Oh, surely not! He was successful and I... I was a nobody.'

She suddenly wanted to smash something. 'I should've kicked up the biggest fuss! But at the time I felt too ashamed and...and I just fled with my tail between my legs.'

'Have you not picked up a paintbrush in all of this time?'

'Of course I have! I've tried many, many times, but my efforts were appalling—so clumsy and awkward...that...' That she'd lost heart.

'His words were still in your head.'

They'd been all she could hear.

Until today.

'And that's why you thought you'd lost your talent.'

'Until today,' she whispered.

'And now you're going to follow your passion and continue painting?'

Yes! Except she couldn't forget that at this moment she was supposed to be Liz, not Liv. 'I mean to take great pleasure in a much-loved hobby again.'

He started to laugh. 'Hobby, huh? I have a feeling that in the not too distant future I'll be losing the services of my favourite office manager.'

She froze. *Dear God!* 'No!' *When had the conversation taken such a drastic turn? Where had she gone so wrong?* She had to make things right again.

Swallowing, she pursed her lips and channelled Liz at her primmest. 'Office work suits me just fine, thank you very much.'

Seb just laughed again. 'You heard what that man was prepared to pay for your painting this morning. All it's going to take is one good exhibition and your name will be made.'

Everything inside her crunched up tight. 'Nonsense. Painting is a hobby, nothing more.'

His eyes never wavered from hers. 'I saw you paint, Eliza. We both know that's a lie.' He moved to stand in front of her, those compelling eyes piercing the depths of hers, and her heart seemed to stop...to hang between beats. 'You've been denying your talent for what...four years?' He cupped her face in his hands. 'Don't you think it's time to follow your dreams?'

His words, his touch, unbalanced her, robbing her of breath. Her hands shot out to grip the sides of his waist, to stop herself from falling into him. The life she'd thought closed to her—the one she'd thought she'd ruined—had magically opened up again at her feet and anything, *everything*, seemed possible.

Heat burned her palms through the thin material of his shirt. Her pulse thrashed and fluttered. It was all she could do not to press closer to that warmth and the intriguing lean firmness of him. She'd bet she'd fit inside the circle of his arms as if she'd been made for them—as if he'd been made for her.

He stared down at her for a long moment. His eyes darkened, but very gently he released her and stepped back. She swallowed and told herself that she was glad.

His phone rang, and he excused himself to answer it. She watched him as he strode away from her down the length of the gallery, phone pressed to his ear. When he disappeared from view she closed her eyes and tried to douse the crazy burning in her blood. He might be the most tempting man she'd met in a long, long time, but she was lying to him. To kiss him would be unforgivable.

It was all she could do not to grab a fistful of hair in both hands and give a silent scream. Dear God, what was Liz going to say? She was making a hash of everything! How on earth was she going to fix this?

Liv retraced her steps to the drawing room and her gaze rested briefly on that awful letter from Seb's father. Damn those parents of his! Seb was honourable. Thank God he was honourable or heaven only knew where they'd be right at this very moment!

She squashed the images that rose in her mind.

The thing was, they had him convinced he couldn't be fun or amusing or…or even interesting. Her mind raced as she made her way back down to the kitchen. 'Mrs Brown, do you know when Seb's birthday is?'

The other woman cocked her head to one side. 'It's in five weeks' time.'

Hmm…that was too far away. She fell into a chair at the table.

Mrs Brown glanced at her. 'Is everything OK, lass?'

She wrinkled her nose. 'Seb has this ridiculous notion in his head that he's not fun-loving.'

The housekeeper raised an enquiring eyebrow.

Her shoulders slumped. 'Look, I know he's not some latent party animal, but…there's more to life than duty and responsibility.' Having a bit of fun wouldn't turn him into his parents.

'That's very true.'

She drummed her fingers against the weathered

wood of the table. 'It's his parents' fault. They have him convinced he's dull and boring.'

Shrewd eyes met hers across the table. 'And you think they're wrong.'

'I *know* they're wrong. And he's just got it all mixed up in his head—responsibility and fun are *not* mutually exclusive.'

In bringing her to Tyrell Hall he'd inadvertently changed her life. For the better. He hadn't set out to, of course, but all the same he was sincerely happy for her. Surely she could return the favour? In a tiny way.

She lifted her chin. He had a poetic soul. And in her experience poetic souls loved a good party. 'Which is why I have a favour to ask.'

Sebastian stomped up to his bedroom. *Dress for dinner?* He scowled. What bee did Brownie have in her bonnet now? Eliza was on his staff, not someone for whom he dressed for dinner. Even if kissing her was becoming harder to resist.

The thought didn't improve his temper.

And none of it changed the fact that *dressing for dinner* was utter nonsense.

He resisted slamming his door—just. He kicked off his shoes and prepared to throw himself down on his bed when he saw the zippered suit bag laid across it with a crisp white envelope resting on top. What on earth…?

He flicked his thumb beneath the envelope's flap and pulled out a one-sided card.

*The Honourable Eliza 'Poppins' Gilmour
requests the pleasure of
Mr Seb 'Elvis' Tyrell's company
this evening from eight o'clock.
For celebration, revelry and shenanigans to
commemorate the return of long-held dreams.
Theme: fancy dress.
Gifts: optional.*

He found himself shaking his head...a slow grin spreading across his face. For a moment he let himself remember the way she'd beamed up at the sky—the momentary joy that had radiated from her. He recalled her heated denials of the accusations his parents had levelled at him. And then the expression on her face when she'd confided her ill-judged love affair with her teacher.

No wonder she was one thing in the office and another out of it. She was living a lie. But it wasn't the same kind of lie that Rhoda practised.

Today had been an extraordinary day for her and she deserved the chance to celebrate. With something akin to dread, he unzipped the garment bag and pulled forth a signature Elvis outfit. He shook his head. She'd remembered the song he'd recited to try to hush Jemima. So...would she dress as Mary Poppins? The thought made him smile.

It might be crazy. It might even be a little dangerous, but she deserved to celebrate and he had no intention of raining on her parade.

He glanced at the card again. It'd been decorated with pictures of balloons and a disco ball—in colour pencils rather than paint, but it still captured her signature style. It'd probably be worth thousands in a few years. Not that he'd ever sell it.

Gifts: optional.

He tapped the card against his hand, thinking hard. In the next moment his brow cleared and he gave a laugh. Perfect.

Half an hour later, Sebastian stood outside the party room—dubbed so by his parents, not Eliza. It ran the length of the entire ground floor of the western wing. He pulled in a deep breath.

You're the only one who can celebrate with her. Don't let her down.

He raised his hand and knocked.

The door was flung open almost immediately and the moment he clapped eyes on her, his jaw dropped. She twirled on the spot. 'What do you think?'

'I…' He could barely form a coherent sentence. 'I thought you'd dress up as Mary Poppins.'

She tossed her hair—well, not her hair so much as the blonde wig that she wore. 'I always had a sneaking suspicion that under Mary Poppins' strait-laced exterior lurked the heart of a vamp.'

'A…' He swallowed again. 'A Marilyn Monroe vamp?'

'But of course, darling,' she said in a breathy Marilyn Monroe whisper that curled around him, making his pulse race and firing an ache of need to life deep inside. 'Is there any other kind?'

Grabbing his arm, she hauled him inside and promptly handed him a glass of champagne. She touched her glass to his. 'Bottoms up, darling.'

She wore a replica of that infamous white halter-neck dress—the one in the photograph where Marilyn stood above the grate—and it outlined her shape to… His mouth dried. It outlined it to utter perfection. He'd never known that beneath her severe suits she had such delectable curves, such generous…

He started when she poked him in the shoulder. 'My dear Elvis, it's far too early to start ogling the hostess. That's reserved for much later in the evening, surely?'

Dear God! 'I'm sorry! I—'

'Relax, Seb.' Her eyes danced. 'We look extraordinary, and probably faintly ridiculous.'

She didn't look ridiculous.

She shrugged. 'It's hard not to stare.'

And then she eased back and did exactly that. Everything inside him went hot and tight as her eyes darkened in appreciation and her lips parted on a sigh. 'Oh, you make a mighty fine King of Rock 'n' Roll.' She grinned and fanned her face. 'Whoa!'

And just like that she removed the last trace of self-consciousness that he felt.

She leaned forward to nudge the bottom of his glass. 'Drink up.'

Colour tinged her cheekbones pink and her eyes sparkled, but whether with delight or from champagne he couldn't tell.

'Come on over and take a seat at the bar.'

He followed her and that was when it hit him— she had the sound of a party coming through the speaker system. He swallowed a grin and pointed. 'You wanted to set the right tone?'

'Oh, the things you find on the internet! Listen to this…'

She was streaming the sound from her tablet and she leaned forward to click a button. The next moment whale song filled the air. She grinned at him and clapped her hands. 'Now we're partying with whales and dolphins. Groovy, huh? Check it out.'

She pushed the tablet towards him before setting out bowls of crisps and nuts. He pushed the item labelled 'Trappist Monks' and the sound of chanting filled the air. They stared at one another before bursting into laughter. 'We'll save that one for the speeches. It has a suitably solemn tone.'

He reached for a crisp. Would there be speeches?

'This one's fun.'

She pointed and he clicked. The sound of fireworks exploding sounded through the room. 'Very...' He searched for a suitable word.

'Loud?' she offered.

'Invigorating,' he said. 'Perhaps we'll save that one for the close of the evening's proceedings.'

'Wise,' she agreed.

They kept playing with the multitude of soundtracks while nibbling on the snacks and sipping at their champagne until he realised with a start that somehow between them they'd finished the bottle.

'I bought you a gift.'

'Oh!' She eased back to stare at him. 'That wasn't necessary. It was just me being silly.'

He pulled the gift from his pocket and handed it to her.

She took it, and then her face turned reverent. *Pride and Prejudice.* Oh, but Seb, this looks like a very old edition.' She gulped, her eyes going wide. 'Please tell me this isn't a first edition.'

'Not a first. A fifth edition from 1902 with illustrations by H M Brock.'

'Who has signed it!' Her fingers moved over the inside cover. 'I'm sure I shouldn't accept this.'

'I'm sure you should. I can't imagine anyone who would treasure this more. You love Jane Austen *and* as an artist you'll appreciate the illustrations.'

'I…' She swallowed and her eyes shimmered. 'I can't believe you remembered that.'

He remembered everything about her. *Dangerous.* He shook the thought away. 'Perhaps it'll remind you of the adventure you once had in an Austen-eque house.'

She stared up at him. 'It's beautiful. It's the best present I've ever received.'

They stared at each other for a long moment, and something arced between them. They swayed towards each other…

But then a knock sounded on the door and both of them jumped back. Eliza pointed to the tablet. 'Choose us some good party music.' And then she went to answer the door.

Recalling the decoration on his invitation, he chose a disco playlist. Disco was silly, fun…not romantic. He gritted his teeth. It set the perfect tone.

'Excellent!'

She sent him a grin over her shoulder as she sashayed to the door and it threatened to undo him completely. He ached to sweep her up in his arms and kiss her, to pull that ludicrous wig from her head and thrust his hands into the softness of her hair and—

'Help yourself to another drink.'

He crashed back to earth to find she'd wheeled in a trolley laden with party food.

'And eat up. Mrs Brown has made enough to feed an army!'

She had champagne, beer and soft drinks on ice. He chose a beer. He ate party pies and sausage rolls, mini spring rolls and meatballs, pigs in blankets and tiny pizzas until he thought he'd burst, while Eliza regaled him with stories of the infamous parties she'd attended at college. There'd been an unofficial school motto—*Work hard; play hard.* And she and her peers had apparently taken a great deal of pride in living up to it.

They played pool on the billiards table—his grandfather would be turning in his grave. She made him dance the twist, and he taught her the jitterbug.

She'd unearthed the karaoke machine and gave an eye-watering rendition of an eighties power ballad. She might be able to paint, but she couldn't sing to save her life. He sang an Elvis medley and she clutched her heart and pretended to swoon.

She dragged him back to the bar. 'You have to make me a cocktail.'

'What would you like?' He'd make her anything she wanted.

'No, no, it doesn't work like that. It has to be a surprise.' She frowned. 'Except, no tequila.'

Right.

'And I'm going to make one for you. We're making original concoctions, you see. And we have to give them appropriate names.'

Uh-huh. He glanced at her from the corner of his eye as she gathered ingredients. Neither of them was drunk, but they were both pretty merry. 'Can I request no cream?'

She beamed at him. 'Of course you can.'

A few minutes later he presented her with, 'A Magnificent Marilyn.' It was a combination of white rum and cranberry juice.

She clapped her hands together. 'It's pink!' She took a careful sip. 'And delicious. Here's yours. It's called, um… Graceland.'

He sampled it. Brandy, a hint of orange liqueur and dry ginger ale. 'Superb.'

She flopped down on the sofa, putting her bare feet up on the coffee table—she'd kicked off her shoes on the dance floor. He eased down beside her and followed suit. 'What happened at your old parties at this point in proceedings?'

Her cocktail floated through the air as she gave an elegant wave of her hand. 'Oh, we'd play ridiculously serious music and lie around being all mellow and artistic and insufferably pretentious.' With mischief alive in her face, she leaned forward to grab her remote. The sound of Trappist-monk chanting filled the room.

He rested his head against the soft cushioned back of the sofa and grinned. 'I thought you were saving that for the speeches.'

'Oh!'

The sofa cushions beside him dipped as she struggled to her feet, and she rested a hand against his thigh for a moment to gain her balance before clambering in her stockinged feet onto the coffee table. She tapped the remote against her glass as if to gain the room's attention.

'Everybody, everybody…if we could have a little hush.'

She'd put the crowd noise back on, but turned it off again now and he couldn't help grinning—her sense of fun was contagious.

'I only want to say a few words. I won't keep you long from your revels. First of all I'd like to thank the wonderful staff here at Tyrell Hall for pulling this event together so seamlessly at such short notice. But most of all I want to thank all of you for coming here tonight to celebrate with me. You have no idea how much it means to me.'

Something in his chest clenched. The smile faded from his face.

'But even more than that I want to thank Seb here for…'

His heart surged against his ribcage. His feet

hit the floor as he shuffled into a sitting position. *For...?*

'For bringing me to Tyrell Hall, because if he hadn't I might've spent the rest of my life not truly living.'

He hadn't done anything!

'And I want to thank him for being so kind and encouraging...and for being the best party companion anyone could ever have.'

His spine straightened when he finally saw what she'd done.

She met his gaze. 'Your parents are wrong, Seb.' A smile trembled on her lips, vulnerability flashing through her eyes. 'You're quite perfect just as you are.'

His heart gave another giant kick. He rose and set her drink to the table beside his before taking her hand and helping her back down to the floor.

And then he folded her in his arms and kissed her.

CHAPTER EIGHT

THE SURE PRESSURE of Seb's lips on Liv's, the way his fingers cradled her head as if she were made of something fine and precious, completely undid her, crumbling any resistance she might've put up.

Resistance? There was no thought of resistance. Kissing Seb was the most exciting, wonderful thing she'd ever done! She flung her arms around his neck and kissed him back with everything she had.

For a moment he seemed to bend under the onslaught of her wholehearted enthusiasm, like a tree in the wind, but he came back with a force that had the potential to fell them both.

'Seb.' His name whispered from her lips. She couldn't help it. She wanted to say his name over and over. She wanted to whisper it to the stars.

Warm lips pressed kisses to her throat, teeth scraping gently across the delicate skin there. Her knees trembled, her legs threatening to buckle beneath her, but his arm slid about her waist to hold her upright…and so very close. She pressed herself even closer. Under her hands, his shoulders flexed—broad and strong. She traced her hands up the strong column of his neck, the stubble on his cheek scraping her palms as she urged his mouth back to hers.

He kissed her so thoroughly, so completely and shockingly explicitly that a fire burst into flaming life and engulfed them both, and all she could do was hold on and try to keep up with him.

Kissing him was like being on a roller coaster. And yet it was like being wrapped in a warm blanket too. It was like flying, but it felt like the most natural thing in the world. Exotic and forbidden scents should be swirling all around them...as well as the scent of baking bread and sunshine-scented soap. She expected to hear fireworks exploding... alongside birdsong. Kissing Seb was all things exciting...and all things warm and welcoming.

It made no sense, and it made all sense.

She fitted into his arms perfectly, as she'd known she would. And she knew that if they were naked they'd fit even more perfectly. And she wanted that. She craved it with every atom, sinew and fibre. Ecstasy sparked to life wherever he touched...and aches and burnings and yearnings. She pressed herself against him to try and assuage the need engulfing her.

'God, Eliza.'

It wasn't his ragged breathing or the hoarseness of his voice that made her freeze. *Eliza.* She wasn't Eliza. She wasn't who he thought she was.

She pushed away from him with all her strength. 'No!'

The single word rang around the room, dispelling her ludicrous notion of fireworks and birdsong. He released her immediately. 'Eliza…?'

She'd let him kiss her when he thought she was someone else. She'd kissed him back. What kind of person did that make her?

She pressed her hands to her cheeks, trying to get her racing pulse back under control. She met those dark, fathomless eyes, her heart pounding so hard it felt bruised. 'This can't happen,' she choked out.

Those smoky eyes narrowed. 'Nothing need happen that you don't want.'

She knew that. Her hands clenched into fists. He'd never force himself on her.

He adjusted his stance. 'Look, Eliza, if you're worried that I've had too much to drink, I can assure you I'm not drunk.'

She wished he'd stop calling her that!

What would you have him call you instead?

She swallowed. 'Neither one of us is rolling drunk. But we've both had more than is wise, and alcohol definitely clouds one's judgement.'

He raised a contentious eyebrow. 'I wanted to kiss you before I had a drink. I've wanted to kiss you for days… And I think you've wanted to kiss me.'

'That doesn't make it right,' she hissed at him, trying to ignore the way her stomach curled in delicious spirals at his words.

'What's wrong with two consenting adults…?' He broke off to drag a hand down his face.

She edged towards the door before she did something foolhardy and threw all caution to the wind. If she did that…it'd be unforgivable. 'Can… can we talk about this in the morning?'

Hooded eyes gave nothing away. He said nothing, just gave a nod.

She turned and fled. She needed to email Liz. She needed to bring an end to this charade as soon as possible. They had to tell Seb the truth.

There was no reply from Liz the next morning.

Liv bit her lip and then seized her phone from the bedside table and dialled her sister's number.

It rang. *Finally!*

And was answered.

'Livvy, I was just going to call you, but…'

Liv dispensed with pleasantries. 'Are you OK?'

'No.'

The tears in her sister's voice—Liz hardly ever cried—squeezed her heart. She leapt up and started to pace. 'Are you safe? Do you need me to call the police?'

'No, no—it's nothing like that. It's just…things are more complicated than I imagined.'

'How?'

'Dear God, Liv, he's an emir!'

She plonked back down to the bed. 'You mean, like an...um, desert king or something?'

'I mean *exactly* like that.'

She couldn't think of a single word to say.

'So you can imagine what a scandal me being pregnant could cause him.'

She frowned. 'You've seen him and spoken to him, haven't you? He's treating you well?'

'He treats me like a princess—nothing is too much trouble. I can't believe how kind he's being. I'm getting the very best of everything—accommodation, food, medical care.'

Her chin shot up. 'Why medical care?' She couldn't keep the sharpness from her voice. 'Lizzy?'

'I've had a little bleeding. It's nothing to be alarmed about but, well, Tariq insists on taking every precaution.'

As he should!

'How are things there with you and Mr Tyrell?'

She gulped. 'Oh, they're fine.' What else could she say?

'Have you found the baby's mother yet?'

'No, but we've a couple of good leads, so we're hoping to solve the mystery soon. Jemima is such a lovely little thing.'

Liz remained silent.

Liv bit back a sigh. 'Lizzy, you're kind and generous and clever and all good things. You *will* make a wonderful mother. I know you don't believe it, but it's true. You just need to have faith in yourself. And if you can't do that then have faith in me and all of the people who care about you and know you.'

'I have to go, Livvy. I can't thank you enough for what you're doing for me.'

Liz disconnected and Liv stared at the phone before falling backwards on the bed to glare up at the canopy. Right, so... Evidently she'd have to keep up the charade for a little longer. At least until she could be assured that Liz's health wouldn't suffer from the shock of finding out how badly Liv had messed up here.

She huffed out a breath and forced herself upright. First things first. She had to get downstairs and relieve Mrs Brown of babysitting duties. If Jemima had had an unsettled night...

She needn't have worried. She found Mrs Brown ensconced in a comfortable chair by the combustion stove, feeding Jemima. Both of them seemed inordinately pleased with each other.

'She was an angel,' Mrs Brown said. 'A delight. We had a lovely time.'

Liv noted the way the older woman smiled at the baby and something in her stomach clenched. As casually as she could, she helped herself to coffee and took a seat at the table. She moistened suddenly dry lips. 'Mrs Brown, I don't suppose you have any…suspicions of where Jemima came from, do you?'

Shrewd eyes glanced up. 'You're thinking that because I'm fussing around the little one like this that I might be her grandma?'

'Oh, no! I—'

'God didn't see fit to give George and I children. It's a shame as we'd have dearly loved a couple of kiddies, but…'

'I'm sorry, I didn't mean to imply anything.'

'It's OK, lass. I'm enjoying playing grandma by proxy. You want to find Jemima's mum and that's understandable and a good thing to be doing.'

What a strange world they lived in. Women became pregnant every day—some of them unexpectedly, like Liz, and some of them with dire results, like Jemima's mother—while other women yearned for the opportunity. It didn't seem fair.

'So if you need to focus on finding the girl who left this baby in Master Sebastian's office, then you need have no fear of leaving the baby with me. I'm more than happy to help.'

Liv bit back a smile. Mrs Brown would evidently be content for Liv to leave Jemima with her all of her waking hours.

'Morning, Master Sebastian.'

She froze. *Look normal. Act normal.* Impossible when her heart was trying to beat a path out of her chest. With a jerky movement she lifted her mug to stiff lips and managed to drink, though she didn't taste a drop.

'You're both up early this morning. But if you give me a tick I'll get your breakfast and—'

'No rush,' Seb assured her. 'I thought I'd take a walk before breakfast. Care to join me, Eliza?'

The sooner they got this over with the better. 'Sounds lovely.' She drained her coffee and rose to her feet.

They walked across the fields in the opposite direction from the co-op towards a copse. They walked in silence and she simply let the peace of the early morning seep into her.

She sensed the moment he turned his head.

'I have a secret,' she blurted out.

As if by prior agreement, they both came to a halt.

'I'm sorry.' She pushed her hair off her face. 'I meant to start this conversation more elegantly, but—'

'I don't care about elegance. I'd prefer honesty.'

She huffed out a laugh. 'And I can't even give you that.'

'You have a secret…?' he prompted.

'Yes…and until you know what it is then nothing can happen between us. Nothing more,' she amended. 'Not that you want a relationship, I know that, but... I mean fling-wise, kissing-wise...nothing can happen.'

Was she really considering having a fling with this man, if they ever sorted this muddle out? She clenched and unclenched her hands. His kisses might be scorching hot, but his heart was on ice. She'd sworn to never get involved with a man like that again.

His hands went to his hips and he stared at a spot in the distance. 'I take it you're not prepared to tell me what this secret is.'

A light breeze lifted a lock of his hair from his forehead. An ache started up at the centre of her. She swallowed and shook her head. 'Not yet.'

His gaze speared back to hers, and there was a fierceness in it that made her mouth dry and prevented her from moving a muscle. 'And this is a secret you believe will matter to me?'

She gave a laugh that held no mirth whatsoever. 'Oh, yes, it's going to matter to you.' She swallowed again. 'I'm sorry, I should never have let you kiss me.'

He swore and swung away, took a few angry strides up the hill before coming back again. 'I promised not to kiss you. I promised to keep things businesslike between us. If I choose to act like my father, then I deserve the consequences!'

'You're nothing like your father!' She tried to

temper her voice. 'Besides, things sometimes just happen.'

He glared at her. 'Like your speech last night! It was so damn adorable.'

Oh!

'It's no excuse, I know that, but… Nobody has ever put themselves to so much trouble for me before.'

Double oh!

She couldn't speak. He traced a finger down her cheek. 'You really can't trust me with your secret, Eliza?'

'I…' She gulped. 'The thing is, Seb, it's not really my secret to tell.'

She went to move away, unable to think when he touched her like that, but his fingers suddenly seized her chin in a relentless grip, forcing her eyes to his. 'Do you know who Jemima's mother is?'

'No!' She stared at him, horrified. 'My secret has nothing at all to do with Jemima. I swear it.'

He nodded and released her, evidently satisfied.

She rubbed her chin, feeling as if he'd branded her. 'The secret was never designed to hurt you. You weren't even supposed to know about it, but…'

'But?'

'But you got to know me. And I got to know you.'

He muttered an imprecation under his breath. 'I

swore never to get involved with another unsuitable woman.'

'I'm… I'm unsuitable?' Her voice wobbled.

He glared at her. 'You have a secret.'

He was right. She nodded and moistened her lips.

He stared up at the sky for a moment. 'Are you married?' He didn't look at her when he asked it.

Her throat closed over. 'No,' she managed to choke out. 'Please don't question me further. I'm not going to say any more.'

'You think I'm going to let this rest?'

His every line was etched in anger and frustration. He seemed to boil with it. It made her tremble—not with fear but excitement.

Still, she couldn't afford to have him digging into her—or Liz's—background. 'Haven't you ever had a big secret, Seb? One that didn't seem so bad at first, but then seemed to grow? A secret you couldn't escape from?'

He dragged a hand down his face. When he pulled it away again he looked haggard. 'I made the mistake of thinking that you and I had become friends. Evidently I was wrong.'

No, he wasn't!

'I think the less time we spend in each other's company, Ms Gilmour, the better.'

With that he turned and strode back towards the hall.

With stinging eyes, Liv set her face in the opposite direction and continued tramping up the hill. What an absolutely rotten time to discover she'd fallen in love with him.

Sebastian knew the very moment Eliza appeared in the doorway of the drawing room. He knew it with a throbbing awareness that travelled up his arms to burn in his chest.

Yesterday she'd done as he'd bid. He hadn't clapped eyes on her for the rest of the day. It seemed he wasn't going to be quite so lucky today. Still, he refused to look up from his laptop. He pretended to be unaware of her presence.

Not that it helped slow the thumping of his heart. He counted the beats that pounded through him while she stood there hesitating on the threshold. He held his breath and waited for her to turn and leave.

The fact she wouldn't trust him with her secret rankled. It made him want to hurl his laptop into the fireplace with all his might.

The night of her party—that ridiculous party— she'd made him feel like someone who mattered.

Yesterday she'd shattered that illusion.

Today…

He ignored the cramping in his chest and continued blindly scrolling through the document open on his computer screen.

Eventually, when he thought he would finally have to turn and stare at her—order her from his sight—she cleared her throat. 'Seb?'

She still said his name as if—

He cut the thought off. 'What?' he barked, glancing up, his blood leaping at the sight of her.

But she wasn't looking at him. She was staring about the room with wide eyes. 'Wow! This looks great!'

Yesterday he and George had moved all the fussy furniture that his parents had favoured out of this room and had replaced it with pieces that had lain dormant and abandoned in far-flung corners of the hall—pieces he remembered from his childhood when he'd taken refuge in rooms far away from his parents. It'd taken them most of the day, but he'd welcomed the distraction.

He glanced around. The room now felt like his. He didn't know why he hadn't done it the moment his parents had vacated the place.

But he didn't need his office manager's approval or the warmth it sent scuttling through him. 'I'm glad you like it,' he drawled in a tone deliberately meant to imply the opposite. 'What do you want?'

'Oh, yes. Sorry.' She swallowed and he couldn't help but watch the line of her throat as it bobbed. 'The thing is, it's occurred to me that...'

Her golden eyes skittered from his to stare at the rug at her feet, leaving him nothing to read except the pallor of her face. His heart clenched at the sight of it. He wanted to tell himself that it served her right. Instead he found himself battling the urge to fold her in his arms and tell her everything was OK.

It wasn't OK.

She had a secret and he was sick to death of secrets, sick to the stomach with the impact they'd had on his life. 'What has occurred to you?' He didn't bark the words, but his voice came out grim and remote. He couldn't help it.

She folded her hands at her waist and stared at his knees. 'It's occurred to me that I'm surplus to requirements here.'

What?

She moved further into the room, her hands clenched tight. 'Mrs Brown is more than capable of looking after Jemima. You and your private investigator are doing all you can to find Jemima's mother.' She lifted her chin and finally met his gaze. 'You don't actually need me here at all.'

He shook his head in automatic denial. 'No.'

'But… I'd be more use to you at the office.'

'No.'

'Why not?'

He widened his stance. 'Have you heard the saying: Keep your friends close and your enemies closer?'

Her eyes flashed sudden fire. 'Am I supposed to be the enemy in this scenario?'

He gave an eloquent shrug. 'Time will tell... once I discover the truth about you.'

Her chest lifted on a sudden intake of breath. 'So all the ways I've helped you and all the things I've done mean nothing?'

They'd meant too much! That was the problem. He needed to find a way to pull back.

She hitched her chin higher. 'You can't keep me here against my will.'

'I've no intention of doing any such thing!' he bellowed.

She took a step back and he tried to moderate his voice. 'Running away, Eliza?'

She sucked her bottom lip into her mouth and stared at him. 'More a strategic retreat,' she finally said.

'I want you to remain here.'

Something flared in her eyes—hope?

'It'll be best for Jemima. I don't want her unsettled any further than she has been already.'

She snapped away from him, strode across to one of the tall windows, but not before he'd seen the light in her eyes disappear. Maybe it'd been cruel of him, but he needed to shore up his defences around her. He needed to keep his wits sharp and honed. Not dulled with desire.

'Will you stay?'

She didn't speak for a long moment. 'For the time being.' She didn't turn around and before he could extract more from her, she gestured outside. 'It appears you have company.'

Footsteps sounded on the stairs and Brownie appeared in the doorway, Jack at her heels. She puffed herself up. 'This...*gentleman* refused to give his name, Master Sebastian, but he insisted on seeing you.'

'Thank you, Mrs Brown, it's OK.' He moved forward, hand outstretched. 'Jack, you have news for me?'

Brownie harrumphed and stomped back down the stairs. From the corner of his eye he saw Eliza stiffen in recognition of the name, and then sit unobtrusively in the window seat...as if she thought he might forget that she was there. As if that were even possible!

'I do have news and I thought you'd want to hear it as soon as possible.'

He motioned the private investigator to one of the sofas. 'You didn't need to deliver it in person.'

'Sometimes it's best. In the interests of privacy.' Jack glanced around at Eliza and then at Sebastian again, raising an eyebrow.

'Jack, this is Ms Gilmour, my office manager. She's been helping me with this...situation.'

'I didn't ring or send an email,' Jack said carefully, 'because there are times when a client might prefer for there to be no record of certain...discussions.'

His heart started to thump. Jack had found out the truth. And it was ugly. He wanted Sebastian to be sure of any potential witnesses to this conversation before they continued.

A part of him was tempted to send Eliza away—as a punishment for her reticence. But he recognised the impulse for what it was—petty and unfair. Her secret, whatever it was, gave her no joy. He was sure of that.

And if he sent her from the room she'd go and pack her things and leave.

He wasn't ready for that. Not yet.

Not ever?

He pushed the thought away.

'Eliza can stay. She can be trusted.'

Her head shot up, but he refused to meet her gaze.

He motioned again to a sofa, taking a seat on the one opposite. 'What do you have for me?'

Jack set his briefcase on the coffee table, snapped it open and withdrew several documents. 'I followed up on the leads you gave me but they didn't prove fruitful. The woman you were concerned about—Rhoda Scott—she's not borne a child in the last six months. And if she had it certainly couldn't be your father's as he's now infertile. He caught a bad case of something nasty five years ago. He's been infertile ever since.'

Sebastian blinked. 'I see.'

'Naturally I continued to follow other lines of enquiry.'

Acid burned the back of his throat. How many other women had emerged from the shadows claiming that Lord Tyrell had fathered their children? Why hadn't they persisted—forced the point with paternity tests and lawsuits? They deserved support—financial *and* emotional support. 'You've discovered that I have...siblings?'

'Your parents have paid two women significant sums to...'

'Keep quiet?'

'Legal contracts were signed. In return for the money the women had to agree to never divulge the name of their child's biological father. Both women had daughters.'

He pushed a folder across to Sebastian. Seb didn't ask him how he'd acquired the information.

'All of the details are there.'

So if he wanted to follow up, make contact with these two half-sisters, then he could.

But would they want to know him?

'Unfortunately, neither woman has a child of Jemima's age.'

So he'd gained two half-sisters in the space of three minutes, but was no closer to discovering the identity of Jemima's mother. He dragged a hand down his face. When he pulled it free he found Jack staring at him, holding out a large A4 envelope.

'I also found this.'

For the life of him, he couldn't reach out and take it. 'What is it?' he croaked.

'A birth certificate.'

His heart leapt. 'Jemima's?'

'Not Jemima's.'

Jack continued to hold it out to him. Swallowing, he took it. His hands were surprisingly steady as he pulled the single sheet of paper from its envelope.

He stared at it. It took him a moment to make sense of the print on the page. His head snapped up. 'You're sure?'

'Yes.'

He slumped back, the air leaving his body in a rush.

'It's all detailed in my report.' Jack set a large packet on the table. Glancing at Sebastian again, he pursed his lips. 'You had no idea?'

He shook his head.

Liv moved across to the sofa, the warmth of her hand on his arm, pulled him back, her golden eyes full of concern. 'Can I get you anything? I know it's early, but maybe a brandy or...?'

He shook his head and wordlessly handed her the birth certificate. She read it and her brow knitted. 'This doesn't make sense. It—'

She broke off, her eyes widening. 'Marjorie Heathcote? Marjorie is your mother's name.'

'Heathcote was her maiden name. She's used her maiden name on that documentation, even though she was married at the time.'

She stared at Sebastian and then at Jack. 'Lady Tyrell gave birth to a daughter just over seventeen years ago? How...how old would she have been?'

'Forty-two,' Jack answered.

She turned back to Seb. 'How old were you?'

'Eighteen.' He'd already calculated it. 'In my last year of boarding school before starting university. I didn't come up to Tyrell Hall at all that year. I spent the summer with a school friend and his family on their estate in Cornwall. My parents spent the summer in Switzerland. I spent Christmas in London.' On his own.

She pointed at another name on the certificate. 'And the father...this Graham Carter?'

'A tennis coach,' Jack said. 'At the time Lady Tyrell became pregnant he was working at the local tennis club.'

'Wow.' She slumped back against the sofa as if all the air had been punched out of her. 'Seb, your parents are seriously messed up.'

She could say that again.

She straightened and glanced at Jack. 'Have you met them?'

He gave an emphatic shake of his head. 'And I don't see that there'll be any necessity for that either.'

'Amen,' she muttered.

For some reason that almost made him smile.

'Lady Tyrell had her daughter adopted?'

He wanted to hug her for asking all the questions he seemed currently incapable of forming.

'She did.'

'Right.' She let out a long breath and glanced back at the birth certificate. 'So this Catherine Elinor Heathcote is Jemima's mother?'

'It appears so. She gave birth to a little girl five months ago in St George's Hospital, and called her Annabelle Jemima Gordon. Gordon is the name of her adoptive parents. It appears they've become estranged. I've been able to trace Catherine to a squat in London. She's living rough.'

'Sad,' Eliza murmured.

They all remained silent for several long moments.

'A sister,' Eliza finally said. She sent Sebastian a sudden smile. 'You have a sister called Catherine and a little niece called Annabelle Jemima. I know it's a shock, but...sisters are great.'

He had a sister... In fact, he had three.

'Well, come on, then.' She dusted off her hands. 'We have a rescue mission to perform.'

CHAPTER NINE

HE STARED INTO her eyes and Liv found it suddenly difficult to breathe. He was staring at *her* again, rather than through her or beyond her, and she wanted him to keep looking at her like that for the rest of her life.

But then the light in his eyes snapped off and he looked away, and a hard stone settled in her stomach.

'You'll stay here and take care of Jemima.' He rose. 'Jack and I will go to the squat and bring Catherine back.'

She folded her arms. 'You do realise you'll scare her half out of her wits? She'll probably bolt. What will you do then? Chase her…kidnap her?'

He swung back with a frown.

She stood then too and did her best to glare down her nose at him, even though he was half a head taller. 'She's a young girl living by her wits— so desperate she left her baby with total strangers. How do you think she's going to react when confronted by two intimidatingly large men storming into her squat, one of whom is insufferably bossy?'

Seb muttered a curse under his breath.

'Even if you manage to prevent her from bolting, you're going to terrify her. And I can assure you that's not the ideal way to build a sibling relationship.'

He glared at her. 'And you think you can help?'

She lifted her chin. 'Of course I can.'

Liv stared at the Fulham address scrawled on the piece of paper in her hand and then at the house in front of them. 'This is it.'

Air whistled out from between Seb's teeth. 'It doesn't look too bad...for a squat.' He switched the engine off and turned to her. 'What's the plan?'

'We go in there and we talk to her. We're non-confrontational. I expect she'll recognise you, but I think you should let me do most of the talking.'

'But—'

'This is an emotional situation for you, Seb, and I understand you want to pick her up and take her away from here as soon as humanly possible.' His eyes darkened at her words. 'But we're not going to railroad her. She needs to feel she has some autonomy...some agency.'

His face twisted and his hands clenched into fists. 'She needs to be away from here and with her daughter!'

'We're not going to bully her. Instinct tells me she's been bullied enough. Do you really want to align yourself in her mind with all the other people she's had to fight against? Do you want her to see you as another enemy?'

'Of course not! I…'

He dragged his hand down his face and her heart went out to him. 'Let's give the softly-softly approach a try first, all right?'

'But if that doesn't work…?'

'Have some faith,' she chided. 'Stop playing the worst-case scenario game.' She studied the photo Jack had provided of a slim girl with dark hair—she looked so young! 'Ready?'

They pushed out of the car, Seb seizing a torch. They were still enjoying bright spring weather and it was only mid-afternoon, but the windows of the house were boarded up and no doubt the electricity had been cut off.

'Have you been in a squat before?' she asked as they picked their way to the front door.

'No.'

'I have.' She didn't knock on the door, but pushed straight in to reveal a cluttered corridor with rooms off either side. A young man—skinny with greasy blond hair that hung past his shoulders—materialised. Liv refused to appear intimidated, even if she had started shaking inside. 'We're looking for Cathy,' she said without preamble.

'Don't know no Cathy.'

She shrugged. 'Katie, then.'

Something flickered in his eyes and she thrust the photo under his nose. 'Small, dark hair…blue eyes.'

He glanced at Seb and back at Liv. He eased back a step as if getting ready to run. 'Who're you? I don't want no trouble.'

'Neither do we. I'm Katie's cousin and he's,' she gestured back behind her, 'my boyfriend.' She held up a twenty-pound note. 'I have a message for her.'

He stared at the money and licked his lips. She couldn't help wondering when he'd last eaten.

'She's out the back.' And then he snatched the money and hustled out the front door. Seb went to grab him, but she shook her head and he let him pass.

'Was that wise?'

'No idea.'

She headed straight for the back of the house. The kitchen was empty but coughing sounded from a room leading off it. Liv followed the sound to a small figure wrapped in a blanket, lying on a dirty mattress on the floor. Seb sent the light from the torch about the room and swore softly.

Liv knelt beside the figure, touched a shoulder through the filthy blanket. 'Katie?'

Eyes sprang open immediately. She stared at Liv and shot upright. 'Is Jemima OK? I left her with you. I saw you go back to the office. I saw you leave with her. You're supposed to be looking after her!'

A fit of coughing overtook her. When it was

over Liv said, 'Jemima is in the best of health. She's a lovely little girl but she misses you.'

The young girl saw Seb and shrank back. 'How did you find me? That woman gave me her word. She said you wouldn't find me here.'

Seb shook his head. 'What woman?'

'She said her name was Rhoda.'

There was that name—Rhoda—again. Liv watched Seb swallow, watched him fight the protective impulse to pick Katie up and take her away from here…watched him fight with some other internal demon.

Eventually he just shook his head. 'We had to find you for Jemima's sake, Katie.'

Katie's face crumpled. 'I can't look after her. I lost my job and…and my adoptive parents wanted me to have her adopted and wouldn't speak to me when I refused, so… Jemima deserves better! I wanted her to be with…family.'

Liv sat back on her heels. 'You deserve better too, Katie. And I think with a little bit of help from your brother, you and Jemima are going to be just fine.'

Katie stared at Seb. Her hands tightened about the blanket. 'You know the truth, then?'

'I only just found out. I had no idea. I wish I'd known sooner.'

Liv heard the suppressed emotion in his voice and wondered if Katie could hear it too.

He knelt down beside Liv and held out his hand. 'I'm Sebastian and I'm very pleased to meet you.'

She hesitated before putting her hand in his. 'I'm... Katie.'

'Look, Katie, I want to take you away from here right now and—'

Liv placed a hand on his thigh. He'd gone into full fix-it alpha mode and Katie's eyes had widened in alarm. 'Seb, it's about what Katie wants rather than what you want.'

'But...'

She watched him struggle with her words, but he finally gave a nod.

'This is what we were thinking, Katie. We thought you might like to come back with us to Seb's London house—it's where we're staying tonight. You can have a bath and we can all eat a nice hot meal...and it might be an idea to have a doctor round to give you a quick once-over, as I don't like the sound of that cough. And then, tomorrow, if you want, we can travel up to Lincolnshire to see Jemima.'

'But...'

'If you want to come back here tomorrow, you can. We'll bring you back any time. It's entirely up to you.'

Beside her, Seb made a strangled noise in the back of his throat. She patted his knee to keep him quiet. They couldn't force the girl against her will.

No matter how much they might want to. If they did that, the minute their backs were turned she'd bolt again. They needed to make her feel safe, and confident that she had some measure of control.

'Katie, this isn't about charity. It's about family.' She leaned in closer. 'And he might not like me saying this, but your brother needs family every bit as much as you and Jemima do.'

Something in Katie's eyes shifted and stilled. 'You have a family?' she whispered to Liv.

Liv nodded. 'I wish everyone could have a family half as wonderful. My sister is my best friend.' She smiled at Katie before hitching her head at Seb. 'I think you'd make him a fine best friend.'

The younger girl's eyes filled. 'Why are you being so nice to me?'

Her throat thickened. 'We all need a hand sometimes. I had one earlier in the week that changed my life. Also, I adore Jemima and I want what's best for her—having her mother there is what'll be best.'

'You think so?'

'I know so. And...'

'And?' she whispered.

'And I care about Seb. I know how much he wants to build a relationship with you and Jemima. It's...it's what friends do—they help each other. So what do you think of our plan, Katie? Would you like to come with us?'

'Yes, please.'

It was the cue Seb had been waiting for. 'I don't mean to frighten you, Katie, but I want to get you out of here and safe and warm as soon as I can.' With that he lifted her straight into his arms.

'Do you want to take anything with you?' Liv said before he could stride with her from the room. If Katie had managed to hold on to any of her belongings it was because they meant something to her. And Liv didn't want to have to come back here ever again.

'My bag!' She pointed to the bag she'd been sleeping with on the mattress. 'And…and would it be OK to leave the torch for the others? It gets so dark in here at night.'

Seb shifted so that Liv could take the torch from his hand. She set it on the kitchen table on their way out. When they reached the car she dug into his jeans pocket for the car keys, trying not to focus on the strength of his thighs beneath her fingers. 'Why don't you sit in the back with Katie? I'll drive.'

'I need to thank you.'

Liv glanced up from what had become her favourite chair in the drawing room—close to the fire, opposite Seb's. It was a wingchair, plush and welcoming, and it fitted her perfectly. She loved what Seb had done with this room, but the peace she'd been seeking was shattered by his presence. His very life force seemed to pulse around her, a blanketing energy that engulfed her whenever he was near.

She unfolded her feet from beneath her and clutched a cushion to her stomach. Her posture probably looked ridiculously defensive, but it meant that her hands were accounted for—busy with other things, like picking at a loose thread. It stopped them from doing something stupid and betraying her. 'You've already thanked me.'

They'd brought Katie to Tyrell Hall two days ago. Jemima had been beside herself with excitement, while Mrs Brown had taken Katie firmly under her wing. And then Katie had told them her story. Mrs Brown had cluck-clucked. Seb had grown grim. And Liv had refused to ask questions. *None of her business.*

According to Katie, a woman once closely associated with the Tyrell family—a woman named Rhoda—had approached her two months previously. She'd handed her a photocopy of a birth certificate—Katie's birth certificate, which had revealed the names of Katie's biological parents. Rhoda had urged her to make the story public and demand financial compensation. She'd told her the family had treated her shabbily and that Katie deserved better. 'She had my birth certificate and my adoption papers. She even had my biological father's death certificate. She seemed to know all about me.'

At the time, Katie had been living in a rented flat with two other girls, but when the flat had been sold they'd been given two weeks' notice to vacate the premises. It appeared nobody wanted to share a house with a baby, and she hadn't been able to find a bedsit she could afford.

Her adoptive parents had given her an ultimatum when she'd become pregnant—give the child up or they'd disown her. They'd had plans for her to follow in their own academically successful footsteps. Rather than a daughter, they'd wanted a carbon copy of themselves. Unable to turn to them for support, on impulse Katie had rung Marjorie.

'Dumbest thing I ever did,' she'd confided. 'She was horrible. She said Rhoda had stolen her private and personal documents and that if I tried to profit from them I'd find myself in serious trouble with the law…and so would Rhoda. I didn't want to profit. I just… I just wanted a family to give Jemima. But she didn't ask me how I was…she didn't want to know me.'

At this point in the story, Katie had buried her face in her hands. A few moments later she'd lifted her head and continued. 'Something about Rhoda frightened me. I knew she was trying to make trouble, but after talking to Marjorie I didn't really blame her. I figured Marjorie had done something awful to her too. Rhoda kept saying they needed to learn a lesson, and that they shouldn't be allowed to treat people so badly. She told me about you, Sebastian. She told me that I deserved to have a portion of what you had.'

She'd bitten back a sob then. 'I didn't believe that. I didn't want your money.'

But it had led her to research the family, and the more she'd read about Sebastian, the more she'd liked him. She'd watched him from afar the last time he'd been in London—just before he'd gone overseas.

'I wanted to approach you, but after speaking with Marjorie I was too afraid to,' she'd confided. 'I was on welfare benefits. I hadn't been able to find a flat. If I'd had a job and proper place to stay, and was doing OK with money and things… well, that would've been all right. But I had nothing and I thought… I thought you'd despise me like Marjorie did.'

Seb had paled at those words. 'I'd have helped you.'

She'd nodded, tears in her eyes. 'I know that now.'

She'd blown her nose and continued. 'Rhoda kept telling me to confront you and demand what was my due, but I couldn't see that you owed me anything. But then Social Services wanted me to come in for an interview and my welfare payments were stopped until I did…and I knew that if they found out I was living rough they'd take Jemima away from me. Rhoda told me that's exactly what they'd do. But she swore if I left Jemima with you, you'd look after her…that you wouldn't go to the authorities because you'd do anything to avoid a scandal.'

At that point Seb had cursed, making them all jump. 'Sorry,' he'd muttered. 'What happened then?'

'She said once I'd done that, she'd help me get back on my feet—find a flat and a job. That it'd be so much easier without Jemima in tow. I didn't want to leave Jemima—I hated leaving her like that—but I was afraid if I didn't do something drastic she'd be taken into foster care and… I couldn't bear it!'

Seb, Liv and Mrs Brown had all assured Liz that they understood, and that they didn't blame her for anything.

Katie had stared up at Seb with those big blue eyes of hers. 'I knew you'd take good care of her. And your secretary had such a kind face. I'd watched her for three days in a row. She bought sandwiches for the homeless family in the park every single day. I knew I could trust her.'

That had made Liv's throat thicken. Seb had turned to her, but she hadn't been able to meet his eyes. 'It was nothing,' she'd mumbled. 'Tell us what you were doing at that squat. Wasn't this Rhoda supposed to be helping you find a flat?'

'I never saw her again after I left Jemima in your office. Not once.'

Seb had nodded, as if far from surprised. 'Rhoda is a malicious piece of work. She wanted nothing more than to cause trouble. She's as bad as Marjorie and Hector. She took advantage of you, Katie, and I'm sorry, but I'm glad it led you to me.'

'I was going to get back on my feet—get a job and find a place to stay—and then I was going to come and see you. But you found me first.'

'I'm glad I did. And now everything is going to be just fine, you'll see.'

Katie was still a little shy around Seb, but it was evident that she had a bad case of hero-worship… and he was slowly but surely winning her trust. He was all she could talk about when she, Jemima and Liv had their daily ramble up to the co-op.

Liv was fiercely glad that Seb finally had a family who looked up to him, who appreciated him the way he deserved to be appreciated, who were going to love him the way he deserved to be loved.

He folded his frame into the chair opposite. 'I haven't thanked you properly.'

She frowned. What did he mean by that?

'When you told me you had a secret that you couldn't share, I acted like a two-year-old and went into a ridiculous sulk.'

Her fingers worried harder at that loose thread. 'It wasn't ridiculous. You were hurt. I totally understood it because we're more—'

She broke off and dug her fingers deep into the plushness of the cushion.

His eyes darkened and he nodded, his eyes never leaving hers. 'Exactly. We're more than just colleagues.'

'Yes,' she whispered.

'But we can't move forward until you deal with this *thing* that you can't tell me about yet.'

She couldn't speak. She could only nod. Though she didn't really know what he meant by moving forward. He'd made it clear that a romantic relationship didn't figure in his future.

Unless he'd changed his mind?

Fat chance! He's talking about sex. Just sex.

She bit her lip, heat flicking through her. But... sex was nice. There was nothing wrong with sex.

But would it be enough?

'It's something you believe can be dealt with, yes?'

'God, yes!' *And soon!* Liz's situation seemed to have reached a more even footing, her health stable. She and Liz had to tell him the truth. Between them all they'd sort the situation out. Beneath the shelter of the cushion, she crossed her fingers.

He stretched out his legs, but she had a feeling his assumed nonchalance was just a front. 'From the very beginning of this strange adventure, you've acted with nothing but integrity, kindness and generosity. Why should I doubt your word now? You tell me you can deal with this unknown *thing* and I'm choosing to believe you. I've no reason not to trust you.'

'Oh!' Her fingers dug so hard into the cushion she was afraid she'd poke holes into it. In the next moment she shot to her feet and flung the cushion back to the chair. 'I… I need to go and make a phone call *right now* and—'

'It can wait.' He motioned for her to sit. 'There's something I want to tell you.'

She sat. She had a feeling she'd do anything he asked of her at the moment.

'You asked me if I'd ever been under the shadow of a secret.'

Her mouth dried. 'Is this about the unsuitable woman you mentioned?'

'Yes.' His lips cracked open the merest fraction to utter that word and Liv's stomach performed a sickening somersault. 'I suspect you've worked it out by now. Her name was Rhoda.'

Her heart stuttered in her chest. 'The same Rhoda Katie spoke of?'

'One and the same. I met her just over three years ago at a business function in London. At the time I didn't question what she was doing there. I know now that she was there to meet well-heeled men.'

Her stomach clenched. 'You started dating?'

'Yes.' The lines bracketing his mouth momentarily deepened. 'She was beautiful, fun…and she played me to perfection.'

Liv's mouth dried. She had no idea what that last bit meant, but it sounded cold-blooded…clinical… awful.

His mouth twisted as if he'd read the confusion in her eyes. 'She discovered my weaknesses and she played on them. I imagine it didn't take her too long to work out what I really wanted, which was a family and a quiet life. So…she turned herself, outwardly, into my ideal woman. And I fell for the charade completely.'

A lump lodged in her throat. He'd fallen in love with her. And then she'd broken his heart and left him completely disillusioned. Even more disillusioned than Brent had left her. At least she hadn't given up on love altogether. She'd always expected to fall in love again one day.

'What I didn't see at the time was that all she wanted was my money and my title.'

She swallowed the lump. It lodged in her stomach, heavy and indigestible. 'How…?' She swallowed again. 'How did you find her out?'

His face had gone grey and he now pressed fingers to his eyes, as if to push back a headache. 'I tried to keep her and my parents separate for as long as I could. I didn't want them tainting the one bright spot in my life.' He gave a harsh laugh, his hand clenching. 'They're snobs, they're unkind, and... I didn't want them to hurt her.'

Her stomach churned. He'd wanted to protect her and she'd obviously thrown it back in his face. Her chin shot up. 'It sounds like they'd have been kindred spirits, bosom buddies!'

His lips lifted into a mockery of a smile. 'Funny you should say that.'

She went cold all over at the expression in his eyes. 'What do you mean?' she whispered.

Sebastian stared at the woman opposite. She was nothing like Rhoda. She'd never set out to seduce a man with one eye always on the main prize. In fact, she'd been doing her level best to do the exact opposite and resist the attraction flaring between them. She'd never use a man the way Rhoda had.

'Seb?'

He opened his mouth and forced the words out. 'Rhoda and my parents hit it off splendidly. So splendidly in fact that I found her in bed with my father.'

He tried to toss the words off lightly, as if none of it mattered any more, but the expression of horror that spread across Eliza's face brought his overwhelming sense of betrayal, and all of the ensuing pain that had ripped through him, to full-bodied life. Rhoda, the woman he'd loved, the woman he'd planned to marry, had betrayed him. *With his father!* A part of him still couldn't believe it.

Eliza stared at him, her face losing all its colour. And then she shot across the small space, dropping on her knees in front of his chair. 'Oh, Seb! I'm so sorry...so very, *very* sorry.'

'She was appalled that I'd found them out.' The sight of their limbs entangled—it was an image he'd never erase from his mind. 'All of her hard work undone in a matter of moments.'

'I can't even...' Eliza trailed off with a shake of her head.

'She begged me to overlook it...she begged for forgiveness...she swore it would never happen again.'

'But you couldn't overlook it,' Eliza said quietly.

'No. I didn't want the kind of *sophisticated* marriage my parents had, but it was clear that's exactly the kind of marriage Rhoda had in mind. And in that moment it was as if the scales had been lifted from my eyes.'

Eliza surveyed him, her face pale, though her eyes were steady. 'Is it too much to hope that she went quietly?'

'It is. She hurled every insult at me she could lay her tongue to. At least she now no longer had to marry the most boring man in England; my father was ten times more fun, et cetera.' If not edifying, it had certainly proved enlightening. 'So she embraced the role of Hector's mistress instead, hoping no doubt to gain some financial benefit from that arrangement…and perhaps some leverage to use against any of us at a later date.'

'Like the documentation she showed to Katie.'

'Exactly.'

His chest clenched and his stomach churned. The episode had left him reeling. It'd left him feeling lonelier than he'd ever felt in his whole damn life.

Eliza's face turned fierce. She gripped his knees. 'She was a liar and a cheat and good riddance to her!'

But then she pulled in a breath and blinked hard—blinking back tears for him, he suspected. 'But I know it wouldn't have felt like that at the time.' She gulped back something that sounded suspiciously like a sob. 'At the time it would've felt as if everything you'd held dear had been ripped away.' She shook her head, her brow creasing. 'How could she have done that to you? How could *he*? That's not an ordinary betrayal it's…so *callous*.'

He'd always known his parents were ruthless and inconsiderate, he'd known he didn't count for much in their emotional landscape, but he'd have never thought his father could break faith with him so completely. It had staggered him. It still did.

The pressure of her hands on his knees pulled him back from the edge of the black pit that opened before him. 'Seb, this is a reflection on them and their warped morals, their...their twisted depravity, not you. You know that, right?'

How could her faith and the vision she had of him temper his pain? He'd never thought he'd be free of it, but something in her face pushed it back and kept it at bay. He didn't understand it. He didn't know whether to be grateful or whether he ought to flee.

She stared back at him as if he were the centre of the universe, and it was all he could do not to take her face in his hands and kiss her until neither one of them could think straight.

He couldn't do that until she told him her secret.

'Do you wish you'd never found out? Do you wish you'd married her?'

He shook his head. 'I'm glad she's out of my life. I'm glad I found out what she was before I made a bigger mistake and married her.' Once they'd married, Rhoda would've worked on getting pregnant as soon as she could. And she'd have wielded that child like a weapon. It made him sick to his stomach thinking about it.

Eliza let out a slow breath. 'What happened afterwards?'

'My parents were living here. *On my charity.* So I threw them out.' He shrugged, fighting an inappropriate grin—not because of the momentary satisfaction it'd given him, but because he knew Eliza would appreciate the gesture.

She stared at him and then her lips lifted in an answering grin. 'Good for you!'

'Part of the settlement—when I extracted my father from his financial straits—was that he and my mother could keep the apartment in Monte Carlo, but everything else had to be signed over to me. They all packed their things and flew there that very day.'

'What?' She frowned. 'Even Rhoda?'

'Even Rhoda.'

'Didn't your mother mind?'

He shrugged. 'She always turned a blind eye to my father's affairs.'

She opened her mouth…and closed it again.

He sympathised. There really were no words to do the situation justice.

'I understand the arrangement between Rhoda and my father lasted for several months before my father tossed her over without a penny. I suspect she'd been trying to get pregnant.'

'Oh, my God! You thought Jemima might be…?'

'That was the phone call I made. I asked her if she'd had a child…that I would make her an allowance if she had. Her reply was a very bitter *no*. She ordered me instead to make recompense for all the anguish she'd suffered at my family's hands. I told her to take a hike and then I had Jack double-check all the facts where she and my parents were concerned. But as my father is now infertile her plan would never have worked.'

'But if it had…' She pulled in a breath. 'She'd have taken your father for all the money she could?'

'Yes.'

'I'd have had no sympathy for him if that had happened, but…'

'But?'

'She'd have had you where she wanted you too, wouldn't she? You'd have done anything to protect that child.'

Exactly. But thank God it hadn't come to that.

'Instead she tried to cause mischief for you through Katie.'

'If she has any inkling how that's ended, she'll be gnashing her teeth.' And it served her right.

Eliza reached up and touched his face. 'And now you need never bother with her again,' she whispered. 'Instead you've gained a sister and a niece who adore you, and who'll look after you.'

He couldn't help it then; he hauled her onto his lap and buried his face in her hair. Her arms went about him and she held him tight. He had no idea how long they remained like that. He only knew that it helped, that it pushed away the darkness that had raged inside him for the last two years.

He eased back to glance into her eyes, and then at her lips—full and plump. They parted a fraction and her breath hitched as if she suddenly couldn't get enough air into her lungs. Adrenaline surged into every muscle, priming him for action.

One of his arms was about her waist, but with his other hand he traced the length of her leg from knee to hip. She shivered and shifted. 'Seb.'

Her voice held a warning note that he ignored as he trailed his hand from hip to shoulder, his hand brushing the side of her breast. She trembled and half smothered an exclamation. Her nipples beaded and peaked through the thin material of her blouse and hunger roared in his ears.

'I told you my nasty little story because you deserved to know it all after everything you've done for Jemima and Katie…and me. Not telling you became too hard.' His voice rasped from him, low and husky…and full of desire.

Her eyes darkened in answer and he felt her press her thighs tight together to counter the same desire he knew coursed through her too.

How had he lived without this for so long—the feel of a warm woman in his arms, a woman he liked and respected…and desired?

'As soon as you sort out this issue of yours, I'm taking you to my bed where—'

Her hand pressed against his lips, silencing him.

'You don't want to make any decisions about me yet,' she whispered.

He trailed his fingers along her collarbone and the delicate skin of her throat, back and forth until her eyes grew dark and slumberous. 'What do you think you're doing?' she finally rasped out.

'One kiss.' He cupped her jaw, lifting her face to meet his. 'One kiss can't hurt.'

Hunger flared in her eyes. 'Seb, I—'

He swallowed her words, his lips closing over hers with a fiercer hunger than he meant them to. She wanted to resist him. He could feel it in the way she tried to hold herself stiff and still. Her hand went to his chest as if to push him away.

He cupped her face in both his hands, his lips moving over hers gently, reverently. He wanted to tell her in a language that needed no words how beautiful he thought her.

A shudder racked her entire frame and rather than push him away, her hand tangled in his shirt to pull him closer as she kissed him back with a vigour that made the blood stampede in his veins.

He lost himself to the sensation and freedom of kissing her. There were no games or hidden agendas—just pure mutual desire and respect, and he revelled in it.

The sound of someone clearing their throat in the doorway had them crashing back to earth.

He dragged his lips from Eliza's, stared into her

stunned eyes, before glancing around to find Katie grinning at him from the doorway. 'Sorry, I didn't mean to interrupt anything.'

'You're not interrupting!'

But Eliza's voice came out on a squeak. She tried to scramble off his lap, but he held her fast, refusing to relinquish her. 'I'm just trying to convince Eliza here that she should date me.'

Katie laughed. 'From where I'm standing, she's looking pretty convinced.'

'Oh, the two of you!' Eliza stopped struggling, and wrestled to hide a smile instead. 'I was taken off guard. You can both just stop it.'

That only made Katie laugh again. The sound gladdened his heart. He had a sister, and a niece... and very soon he meant to have Eliza.

'I just popped my head in to say goodnight.'

'Goodnight, Katie.'

'Sleep well,' Eliza called after her.

She turned her gaze back to Seb. He wanted to kiss her again, but he didn't trust that he'd be able to stop. He reached up to wind a lock of her hair about his finger. 'I do want to date you, Eliza. I hope you'll agree.'

She swallowed.

'We'll take it slowly.' He wanted to get it right this time.

She folded her arms and lifted her chin. 'Whenever a man says he *wants to take it slowly* that just means he wants to take the emotional commitment slowly. He still usually wants to jump into bed as soon as possible.'

He stared at her, fighting a scowl. *What on earth...?*

She sent him a smile that held a world of hurt... and he hated that he might have somehow put it there. 'Guilty as charged, huh?'

He thrust out his jaw. 'I want you physically. I have no desire to deny it. As for the rest...' He lifted a shoulder and let it fall. 'It's too soon to know.'

She nodded, but whether in agreement or not he couldn't be sure. Why did women always want assurances and promises? He could give her neither.

This time when she scrambled off his lap, he didn't try to stop her.

Soon, he told himself. Soon.

With a growl of frustration, Liv threw her phone to her bed. Why did Liz have her phone turned off *still*?

Seizing her laptop, she checked her emails. There was nothing from Liz. Pulling in a deep breath, she started typing.

Dear Liz,
I've fallen in love with your boss.
I'm sorry, I didn't mean to.

I need to tell him the truth.
Please get in touch with me asap.

She signed off and waited.

And waited.

She didn't fall asleep until the wee small hours.

She woke in the morning to her ringing phone. She glanced at the screen—*Liz*! She pressed it to her ear. 'Where have you been? I've been trying to contact you for days! I—'

'Oh, Livvy, I'm so sorry! Have you seen today's newspapers?'

'No, why…? I've only just woken up. Hold on…' She grabbed her laptop, turned it on and then scanned the newspaper headlines, her heart dropping like a stone to her stomach. 'Oh, God.'

Had Seb seen these yet?

She shook herself. 'Is it true?'

'Um…yes.'

'You're engaged?'

'Look, it's complicated. I'll explain later, but first you need to get to Sebastian and tell him the truth before he sees these headlines.'

Dear God, Liz was right!

'Good luck, Livvy.'

She had a feeling she was going to need it. 'I'll ring you later.'

CHAPTER TEN

LIV THREW ON the nearest clothes to hand. She tried
Seb's room first, but received no answer to her
knock. The room was empty. She started for the
kitchen but redirected to the drawing room first.

He glanced up the moment she entered. She
saw the newspaper open in front of him—with the
news of Liz's engagement to King Tariq splashed
all across it.

She covered her face. Why hadn't she followed
her instincts and told him the truth last night?

She pulled her hands away. 'I was hoping I'd get
a chance to explain before you saw that.'

'You can explain this?'

The coldness in his voice made her recoil. 'Yes,'
she replied, but her voice barely emerged above a
whisper.

'If this—' he lifted an edge of the newspaper '—
is Eliza Anne Gilmour, former office manager of
the esteemed Tyrell Foundation,' he quoted, 'then
who are you?'

She wanted to go and sit beside him, but his
coldness forbade it. She twisted her hands together.
'I'm Olivia Grace Gilmour, born twenty-two minutes after Eliza Anne. Liz is my sister…my twin
sister.'

He stared at the paper rather than at her—as if the sight of her disgusted him.

She swallowed. It wasn't disgust. It'd be too easy for her to hide behind that, to get all uppity and defensive and use it as an excuse to fight against his reaction. It wasn't disgust that he was experiencing, but betrayal and pain. This lie had hurt him. As she'd known it would.

Oh, she hadn't known that at the beginning, of course. But she *had* known it since they'd had such fun together at their private party…*since that kiss.*

And yet you still didn't tell him the truth.

Which made her a fool!

He still refused to look at her and panic clawed at her belly. She pressed her hands to her stomach and tried to keep it at bay. With him refusing to look at her, she wasn't sure what to say next…or what to do.

'I'm sorry.' She couldn't keep the emotion from her voice. She didn't even try to.

She hesitated and then perched on the sofa opposite, her knees shaking. She gestured at the newspaper. 'Eliza—Liz—met King Tariq on her holiday to Greece. She didn't know who he was— he was travelling incognito—but they had a holiday romance. It wasn't until Liz was back home in London that she found she was pregnant.'

His head lifted, but not an ounce of warmth filtered across his face. 'That's why she asked for more leave—to find him and tell him that they were expecting a child?'

'Yes.'

His hands clenched and his eyes blazed in his face. 'Why didn't she tell me the truth?'

She tried not to flinch at the accusation ripping through his words. 'Because the two of you are as reticent as each other.'

He shot to his feet. 'So this is my fault?'

'Of course not!' She shot upright too. 'But, just for a moment, look at it from her point of view. She was scared witless at finding herself unexpectedly pregnant. And she was frightened of losing her job.'

'I would never—'

'And she wasn't thinking as clearly and logically as she'd have normally done.'

He gave a harsh laugh. 'So she called on you for help.'

She couldn't stand it any longer. She raced around the coffee table to stand in front of him, so close waves of heat beat at her. She ached to touch him, but she didn't dare. 'The switch wasn't even supposed to have an impact on you.'

His jaw dropped. 'Not have an impact…?' And then he ground his teeth together so hard she winced.

'You were overseas…and Liz was only supposed to be away for a few days. My role was to simply keep the office running smoothly until she came back—something I am actually qualified to do, by the way. We had no intention of defrauding you. And Liz had every intention of being back before you returned.'

'But your nasty little scheme didn't go to plan.'

She swung away, strode to the window. 'There was nothing nasty about it. We weren't trying to steal from you or rob you. Your office was being taken care of…and you were never supposed to know—what you don't know isn't supposed to hurt you, right?' *Wrong.* 'It wasn't supposed to hurt anyone!'

She turned back. How naïve that all seemed now. 'But Tariq's being a king complicated everything. Then there were plane strikes…and an anonymous baby was left on your desk.'

He strode across to her, his eyes flashing silver fire. 'The scheme turned nasty the moment I kissed you and you still didn't tell me the truth.'

She swallowed and nodded. 'Yes.' She hated being so far in the wrong, but she hated the fact that she'd hurt him more. 'It was wrong of me… really wrong.'

'I understand your wanting to help your sister. I can even understand your agreeing to stand in for her at the office, but the rest of it…' He shook his head.

He stared at her as if he didn't know her, and

that stung. 'The only thing I lied about was my name,' she whispered. 'Everything else was the truth.'

He gave a laugh so devoid of mirth that nausea burned the back of her throat. 'You expect me to believe that?' And then his eyes went horrifyingly blank. 'You're just as bad as my parents. You're just as bad as Rhoda.'

'That is not true!' Fear and anger swirled through her, making the edges of her vision darken.

'I want you to pack your bags and go back to London. I never want to see you or your sister again.'

No! She pulled in a breath. 'I know you feel betrayed and hurt, Seb, and I don't blame you. I know you're angry at the moment, and rightly so. I know what I did was wrong—big-time wrong. But are you really going to throw away what we could have because you refuse to give me another chance? I swear I'll make this up to you. I swear I'll never let you down like this again.'

She held her breath. He'd made her no promises last night. That had been painfully clear. But he had at least been willing to explore the potential for something more.

'What we could have?' He raised a mocking eyebrow. 'My dear Ms Gilmour, a few pleasant kisses does not a relationship make.'

The words were designed to draw blood...and

they did. But she lifted her chin. 'It was more than that and you know it.' Her hands clenched. 'If all we'd shared was nothing more than *a few pleasant kisses*, you wouldn't be feeling this cut up now.'

His nostrils flared. 'I do not envisage a future with a woman who has lied to me about her very identity.'

Which is why he was trying to cast her in the same mould as Rhoda and his parents. Well, she wouldn't let him! She reached out and placed her hand over his heart. He stiffened, but he didn't move away. 'I know you in here, Sebastian Tyrell. I know the real you.' He paled at her words. 'And you know me in exactly the same way, regardless of whether you call me Eliza or Olivia.'

His eyes, dark and hard, bored into hers. 'It's not what it feels like. It feels like I don't know you at all. It feels like I never did.'

The words emerged from white lips and she reefed her hand back, her heart pounding, hope lying in tatters at her feet. 'I love you.' She hadn't meant to say the words out loud, but now that she had she didn't try to retract them.

'I'm sorry, but I'm going to go with my gut instinct on this one.'

Her words hadn't penetrated even a millimetre beneath the armour he'd wrapped securely about him.

'I'm afraid my idea of love is different from

yours. As soon as you have your bags packed George will take you to the station.'

She swung away to stare blindly out of the window. She'd wrecked everything.

She listened to him walk away, but he paused in the doorway. 'How could you be persuaded to do something so deceitful?'

She swung around, her fists clenching. 'You were too!' If he wanted to see the world in such black and white terms she'd give him a dose of his own medicine. 'You kept Jemima's plight from the authorities.'

'That's nowhere near as bad as you lying about your identity!'

'You can only say that because you weren't caught!'

They met in the middle of the room like combatants, both of them throwing any veneer of civility out of the window.

She thrust her chin out. 'Why is what I did worse than what you did?'

'Because I had Jemima's best interests at heart,' he bellowed. '*You* didn't have *my* best interests at heart.'

'Oh, and what do you think a judge would make of that defence—*I had the baby's best interests at heart, Your Honour*—if Katie had panicked and reported that you'd kidnapped her baby...or if she'd never been found and the authorities discovered you were harbouring an unknown child? Huh? *Huh?*'

She stood on tiptoe as she *huh*-ed him, straining to meet him eye to eye. No doubt later she'd die a thousand deaths at her childishness, but for the moment she'd lost all semblance of control.

He opened his mouth, but it took several moments before words emerged. 'That didn't happen! You're creating hypothetical scenarios based solely on their dramatic impact—'

'The police, a judge, all of those people wouldn't consider it any defence at all. As for hypothetical situations, well here's another one for you. What if I'd told you the truth last night?' As she'd been so tempted to do. 'Would you be feeling like this now?'

His eyes narrowed. 'But you didn't tell me last night and—'

'You got lucky! I didn't!'

She shouted the words. She shouted them more loudly than she'd ever shouted anything.

They stared at each other, both breathing heavily.

'You got lucky with Katie, but I didn't get lucky with you.'

He didn't say anything, not that she expected him to see their situations as in any way similar. The shouting felt good. Although she knew it was only a temporary panacea. Still, it was better than dissolving in a flood of tears at his feet.

'And I'll tell you something else—' she jutted her chin aggressively again and hoped it hid the way her bottom lip wobbled '—I've helped you a whole lot more than I've harmed you.'

His face set in mutiny but she refused to give him a chance to speak. 'Liz wouldn't have been able to cope with an abandoned baby. You're lucky you got me instead.'

'What the hell—?'

'Yes, lucky! Liz would've called the authorities like any sane person would've done…except I was *persuaded* to do otherwise.'

He blinked.

'And I expect a defence of "I did it because my boss asked me to" wouldn't hold much water with the authorities either. Were you thinking of *my* best interests in that situation?'

The tightening of his mouth told her that arrow had found its mark.

'And I stopped you from making a hash of things with Katie and scaring her out of her wits, which now means you're getting the chance to form a decent relationship with her.'

He stared at her, his eyes throbbing, but he remained tight-lipped and all the fight left her. Still, she refused to let her chin drop. 'I was trying to help my sister—a sister I love. Why on earth do you think you deserve my loyalty over her? I've known her all my life and I've known you for all of five seconds.' She folded her arms. 'You can remain as cold and distant and unbending as you want, but I know the truth.'

'And what truth is that?'

'That I *have* helped you, Seb.' She moistened her lips. 'And that I am deserving of your forgiveness.'

He didn't say a word and her last hope died. She'd been so sure that he'd *liked* her—that their souls had understood each other on a primal level—and that what they'd shared had been more than a physical attraction. But maybe that had been a chimera, wishful thinking on her part, because if he had truly *liked* her, then surely she should be able to reach him.

She pressed a hand to her brow. 'Is there anything else you want to say, other than goodbye?'

His lips cracked open briefly. 'No.'

The room blurred. 'Right, I'll go and pack my bags then.'

She turned and left. She pulled in a breath. She would not cry. She pulled in another breath. She would not cry. She pushed all the pain to the periphery of her being. She'd try and find a way to deal with it when she got home.

Her phone rang. On automatic pilot she pressed it against her ear. 'Hello?'

'Livvy, how are you? How did things go with Sebastian?'

Don't laugh. She had a feeling that laughing would open floodgates she'd not be able to close again in a hurry. 'Oh, about as well as either one of us expected. I'm sorry, Liz, but you've been fired. I can't talk now. I'll call you tonight.'

She rang off, found her suitcase and started throwing her things into it.

'As soon as Ms Gilmour is ready I want you to drive her to the station.'

The four occupants of the kitchen—Brownie, George, Katie and Jemima—all snapped to attention at his sergeant-major tone. Newspapers littered the kitchen table and he wanted to collect each of them up and shove them into the wood-burning stove.

Except that'd reveal the extent of the storm raging through him, its ferocity.

He wanted to open his mouth as wide as he could and yell with all his might. But what good would that do? It'd only frighten everyone.

'Very good, Master Sebastian.'

His back teeth ground together. For God's sake, why couldn't they just call him Seb the way Eliza did?

Her name isn't Eliza!

The formality isn't their fault.

Don't take this out on them!

He shot one last blistering glare at the newspapers and then made for the door. 'I'm going for a walk!'

He left before anyone could say anything. Questions would be asked and explanations would need to be given, but he didn't have the heart for it at the moment. Maybe after lunch...or tomorrow... next week.

To hell with it. Maybe he'd shut the topic down—declare a ban and order a blanket of silence on it.

It's not curiosity. They care.

The voice that echoed through him sounded suspiciously like Eliza's. He stopped and braced his hands on his knees, drew in several deep breaths.

I've helped you more than harmed you.

He shot upright and surged forward again, his legs eating up the distance between the house and co-op buildings. He veered to his left and vaulted the fence, making for a copse at the top of the hill. He didn't want to see anyone. He didn't want to speak to anyone.

She'd lied to him and the size of the lie made his chest constrict until he could barely breathe— as if a giant hand had reached out and wrapped about his middle and was trying to break him. He couldn't ignore the pain. He just did his best to breathe through it.

When he reached the top of the hill, he was breathing hard and cramping all over. He threw himself down onto a fallen log and rested his head in his hands.

I love you.

His head jerked up, pain knifing behind his eyes. What kind of love lied so...completely? He'd started to believe...

He was a fool!

When he'd found Rhoda with his father, it'd horrified him. But Eliza's duplicity devastated him to a whole new level that he didn't understand. She hadn't just lied about what she'd done. She'd lied about who she was.

And yet, even now, he wanted to believe in her. What kind of fool did that make him?

'What the hell?' He shot to his feet only to see Naomi—one of the co-op's artists—marching up the hill towards him.

She stopped about twenty feet away when she realised he'd seen her. Keen eyes scanned his face and then she moved the last few paces towards him. 'I saw you trekking up here and I came after you.'

'Why?' He didn't mean to sound unfriendly, but he couldn't help it. Did everyone at the co-op know he'd been played for a fool too? Had they all read the newspapers this morning, seen that his former PA was now engaged to King Tariq? Had they joined the dots of a complicated deception, just as he had?

'There's something I think you should see.'

He set off back down the hill. 'I'm not in the mood.'

'I wouldn't have troubled you if I didn't think it was important.'

He halted and glared at her.

She didn't betray by one flicker of an eyelash what she was thinking. 'I wouldn't have troubled you if I didn't think you might...regret not seeing this.'

He huffed back a growl of pure frustration. 'Fine!'

Without another word, Naomi led him down the hill and into the main co-op building...up the stairs to the mezzanine level. She didn't try to engage him in conversation, evidently sensing his current aversion for idle chitchat. Not that it'd take a rocket scientist to work that one out.

She led him out to the artist's workspace and gestured to a painting awaiting framing. There was no denying the identity of the artist.

Eliza.

His hands clenched. *Olivia Grace Gilmour.*

The picture was of the hall's kitchen garden. It was bright, vibrant and pulsing with energy.

'She's donated this to the co-op. She's requested

that the proceeds be split between the co-op and the Tyrell Foundation charity.'

He turned to stare at her. 'When did she organise that?'

'Earlier in the week.' She glanced back at the painting. 'It's a handsome gift.'

His mind whirled.

'She's promised us a new painting every year for the next five years. It'll put this place on the map.'

Why? Why would she do such a thing?

Balm to a guilty conscience?

But... That didn't ring true. She hadn't known earlier in the week that this situation would explode in her face.

He recalled her jubilation—her elation—at painting again. He closed his eyes. Gratitude—she wanted to thank them...wanted to share that jubilation and joy with them.

It was part of who she was.

He rolled his shoulders. As well as being a liar.

His heart started to thump against the walls of his chest. How different would he be feeling today if she *had* told him the truth last night?

But she hadn't...

'The painting I really wanted to show you is over here.' Naomi halted in front of a large easel covered in a dust cloth. She hesitated. 'I hope I'm doing the right thing...'

And then she pulled the cover free. Everything inside of him froze.

It was a picture of him.

Olivia had painted him.

And the impact of the image had him rocking back on his heels. In the painting he held Jemima against his chest, but the baby had turned to stare up at him—wonder alive in her eyes. While he… He gulped. In that painting he looked alive and animated and full of plans for the future.

And yet the picture was deceptive, its mood shifting and changing as he moved in front of it. At certain angles the lines of his shoulders reflected a restless energy rather than relaxation. The lines of his mouth that appeared at first glance soft took on an edge that looked almost…carnal. He ran a hand across his chest to try to ease the tightness there.

In the painting he wore one of his white business shirts, and it should look starched and professional. Instead it hugged the outline of every muscle he possessed and a fleeting impression of intense sexuality sizzled across his eyes…gone again in a flash…and then there again.

She'd made him look raw and vital and beautiful. And complicated, protective and desirable. All at the same time. He sure as hell didn't look boring.

His heart beat hard. He was missing something. The painting was trying to tell him something. But what? He moved a few paces to his right and then his left. He moved in closer and then eased back out, never once taking his eyes from it.

'She's left instructions for this to be delivered to you on your birthday next month.'

She'd promised him a painting.

And she'd kept her word.

And that was when he saw it. From a certain angle Jemima's eyes looked like Eliza's eyes— *Olivia's* eyes.

Blood drummed in his ears. Was that baby Jemima at all…or a child she'd imagined having with him?

Did Olivia look at him—view him—with the same sense of wonder that the baby did?

The only thing I lied about was my name.

The truth of those words felt like a physical lessening of all the tension inside him—a letting go of anger and pain and the bitterness of disappointed hopes.

What right did he have to judge her so harshly, to be so fiercely angry with her, when he hadn't made her a single promise? He hadn't given her any assurances. He hadn't hinted at how much she'd started to mean to him. Why not? Because he'd hidden the truth from himself. He hadn't been honest with her, so how could he blame her for keeping her sister's secret? He'd given her no incentive to do otherwise!

He turned and left the studio at a run, clattering down the stairs and heading for the hall. Had George already left with her? He crossed his fingers and hoped his interfering sister and bossy housekeeper had insisted she needed to eat first, had delayed her with surreptitious questions. He put his head down and ran faster.

He was breathing hard when he approached the back door. Relief, when her voice drifted outside to him, made him sag while he tried to catch his breath.

'Look, none of this is Seb's fault, and you aren't to give him a hard time about it.'

She was defending him? He shook his head.

'He's an idiot if he lets you go.'

That was Katie and he could picture the outrage on her face.

'You've helped me and Jemima *so* much.'

'And so has he. Please, Katie, he's not to blame for this. It's my fault. I lied to him, and hurt him.'

'Ah, but lass, you didn't mean to.'

'It doesn't change the fact that I did, though. I don't blame him for not forgiving me. I don't think I'll be able to forgive myself.'

OK, enough. He refused to let her suffer a moment longer. She *had* helped him—more than he'd ever had the right to expect. She'd given him everything that she had to offer and he had no intention of throwing it back in her face.

'You will come to the party, won't you?'

He faltered, one step from the door. What party?

'I mean, you're the one who's organised it. And he won't still be angry with you by then. He'll have got over it.'

'Oh, Katie, it's really not the kind of surprise I was aiming for when I suggested we throw him a surprise party.'

She was giving him a party?

He surged into the kitchen. They all turned to look at him, but he only had eyes for Eliza.

Her mouth dropped open. She snapped it shut and then chafed her arms. 'I'm sorry, I meant to be gone before you got back.'

She wasn't going anywhere, but he didn't want an audience for all the things he wanted to say to her. Reaching forward, he seized her hand and pulled her out of the door and all the way into the walled kitchen garden.

He could identify each and every plant she'd painted.

'Seb, what do you think you're doing? I think we've yelled at each other enough and—'

He spun her around, seized her face in his hands and kissed her. He wanted to be gentle, but he felt too much like the picture she'd painted of him—restless, primal and filled with need.

Her lips yielded beneath his, a moan dragging from her throat, her hands clutching fistfuls of his shirt to keep her upright.

He lifted his head to stare down into her dazed eyes. She unclenched her hands from his shirt, smoothed out the material and ran her tongue over her swollen bottom lip. 'I…' Her throat bobbed as she swallowed. 'I couldn't read that kiss at all.'

Because she was afraid. Just as he'd been too afraid to see the truth earlier.

Liv stared up at Seb and her heart pounded so loudly that for a moment she couldn't hear anything else. A wild hope tried to spring free, but she roped it back down. He might not be as furious with her as he had been an hour ago, but it didn't mean…well, it didn't mean he ever wanted to see her again after today.

She shook her head. 'You don't like me any more. You hate me.'

'I don't hate you.' He stared down at her with those grey eyes that seemed to pulse with an inner light. 'I just saw the painting you've donated to the co-op.'

'Ah.' She clasped her hands together and tried to ignore the burning in her chest. That'd explain why his anger had abated. It explained why he didn't want to part from her on such unpleasant terms. 'It was the least I could do. Naomi, Dirk and Helen have helped me so much. It's just a small thank-you.'

The light in his gaze smouldered and sparked,

and she tried not to read too much into it. Her paintings had often filled viewers with an enthusiasm that searched for immediate release. That was all this was now. Plus, Seb was the kind of man who always took the time to thank others, to let them know when a gesture was appreciated.

Beneath all of that he'd still be wrestling with his anger. Not that she blamed him.

'I also saw the picture you painted for my birthday.'

'Oh!' Wow. OK. She took a step back and lifted her chin. She didn't ask him if he liked it. 'Did you see anything in that painting?'

His eyes darkened. 'I saw the truth.'

'What truth?' She wanted her voice to come out strong and unflinching, but it didn't. It came out the exact opposite. She wanted to turn and run away, but his eyes held her captive.

'I saw that you loved me.'

A lump lodged in her throat. 'I've already told you that.'

'I was humbled when I finally let myself see how you saw me.'

Very slowly, she nodded. 'Good.' It was better than nothing, and probably more than she deserved.

'I realised, despite all of the other confusions going on, you never hid your real self from me.'

Everything inside her stilled. She felt as if the

smallest breeze might knock her over. She couldn't speak. She couldn't do anything except stare at him.

'I realised it didn't matter if your name was Eliza or Olivia or Rumpelstiltskin.'

That was the moment when she finally started to hope...and when she recognised at least a part of what emotion lay in those smoky eyes of his. She took a step towards him. 'You...you *don't* hate me.'

A smile hooked up one side of the mouth that had become so dear to her. 'I've already told you that.'

Her pulse kicked up a notch as she continued to read his eyes. 'You *like* me.'

'Olivia Grace Gilmour.' He took her face in his hands and his touch was like water to a thirsty plant. 'I love you.'

He loved her?

He loved her!

She pulled his mouth down to hers and kissed him with everything she had—with every crazy emotion roiling through her body.

When he lifted his head, long minutes later, his eyes were dark and ravenous. He traced a finger down the vee of her shirt, sparking a path of fire that arrowed to her centre. 'I hope you don't have plans for the rest of the day.'

'Oh, I have plans all right.' She tossed her head. 'But they all include you.'

For a moment she thought he was going to sweep her up in his arms then and there and stride up to his room. She burned at the thought.

Instead he towed her across to a garden bench and pulled her down onto his lap. 'I want to apologise for my anger earlier.'

She smoothed her hand down his cheek, relishing the scrape of his stubble against her palm. 'You were entitled to your anger, Seb. I don't blame you for it.'

'I refused to listen to reason, I refused to trust you and—'

'Oh, but—'

He pressed his fingers to her lips. 'Let me finish.'

She pressed a kiss to his fingers before nodding. His eyes darkened, but he didn't kiss her. She understood why. He wanted to explain and she needed to hear what he had to say, to understand. Before their relationship moved to the next level, they had to make sure that there were no more barriers or misunderstandings—that the air was clear and the path at their feet unobstructed.

'You've heard the stories about my parents. You know what Rhoda did.'

Her heart ached for him. She'd give him so much love it'd make up for the pain of his past.

'So you'll understand what I mean when I tell

you that my default position whenever receiving unpleasant news is set to disaster mode.'

She thought about that. It made sense. 'You immediately leap to the worst-case scenario?'

His lips twisted. 'Where my parents are concerned that attitude usually saves time, heartache and money. With them I've learned not to expect or hope for any extenuating circumstances.'

How old was he when he'd learned that lesson—twelve? Ten? Even younger? She pressed a hand to his cheek. 'I'm sorry.'

He covered her hand with his own. 'It's not your fault, sweetheart.'

Her toes curled at the endearment. He was a wonderful man with a huge heart. He only deserved the best life had to offer. 'So this morning when you saw the newspaper headlines you immediately leapt to the conclusion that...' Her heart squeezed tight. 'That I'd taken you for a ride, taken complete advantage of you, and that I'd lied about everything.' She pulled in a breath. 'You must've thought I didn't have an honest bone in my body.'

'I couldn't think straight.' His eyes throbbed with remembered pain and confusion, and she wished she could wipe it away. 'I lashed out at you, too afraid to believe anything you said.'

'I'm sorry,' she whispered.

He lifted his head. 'And then I saw the picture

you'd painted of me and I realised you'd never meant to hurt me.'

He traced a finger across her cheek making her blood leap. 'In that moment I understood that your sister had put you in an untenable position.'

'She didn't mean to.'

'And that I'd put you in an untenable position too. Not informing the authorities of Jemima's situation could've backfired badly…and yet you chose to trust me and to help me—to help Jemima—because that's the kind of person you are. You have a heart of gold, Olivia Grace Gilmour, and I love you.'

Her chest filled until she thought it would burst.

'If I'd told you that sooner, you'd have told me the truth.'

She dragged in a breath and blinked hard. 'I love you, Seb. But I do understand if you want to take things slow.'

He shook his head. 'I don't want slow. I just want you.'

She had to pinch herself.

He grinned down at her and she had a feeling he felt as light and free as she did.

A smile burst to life inside her. And then she pulled his head down for a kiss that sealed every silent promise their hearts had just made to each other.

EPILOGUE

One year and five weeks later...

A FAMILIAR HEAT radiated through Sebastian when Olivia came up behind him and slid her arms about his waist, resting her chin on his shoulder. For a moment they both silently watched the revels taking place in front of them.

'Surely *this* is your favourite party?' she said, pressing a kiss to his cheek. 'Though…it has to be said…we did have a rather fine party for our wedding.'

They'd married five months ago. 'We did,' he agreed. 'And this too is a very fine party.'

She frowned up at him. 'But?'

His smile grew. 'But nothing will ever top our Marilyn and Elvis party.'

She tossed her glorious autumn-toned hair. 'I mean to make it my life's work to eventually throw you a party that bests it, you know?'

Impossible. That was the night of their first kiss. The night he'd fallen in love with her. Nothing could ever beat that. 'I look forward to it,' he said instead. It might not be possible to beat it, but he meant to enjoy the ride.

He still couldn't believe he'd come to love parties so much, but he'd discovered a party with Olivia by his side was a thing to be cherished. He half turned so he could slide an arm about her shoulders and draw her closer to his side. 'And I promise you that I'm loving my birthday party tonight.'

She smiled and pointed. 'You're not the only one. Philippa is having a grand old time.'

At thirty, Philippa was the oldest of his half-sisters and a mischievous extrovert, not to mention an outrageous flirt and confirmed bachelorette. The two of them were complete opposites and yet they'd hit it off splendidly. Currently she was holding court in a circle of half a dozen of the most eligible bachelors in England. He couldn't suppress a grin. 'No surprises there.' He searched the room. 'What about Laurie? Please tell me she's not hiding in some dark corner.'

'Of course not. She's in earnest conversation with a group in the room next door. They're playing cards but it's just a pretext to discuss politics.'

Laurie was his middle sister, much quieter than Philippa and shyer than Katie. They were getting to know each other—slowly. More slowly than he'd like, perhaps, but he was grateful to have her in his life and he suspected she felt the same.

He sent up a silent prayer for the information Jack had been able to unearth. And another for the fact that his sisters had agreed to meet him, and had agreed to become a part of his life.

His youngest sister's laughter reached him from the nearby billiards table. As there were eight of them playing they'd obviously made up a new set of rules for the game. 'It's been great having Katie and Jemima down for the weekend. I've missed them.'

Olivia pressed closer to his side. 'Me too, but she's so happy.'

Two months ago Katie had taken up an administration position at the Tyrell Foundation when Judith retired. She had plans to take over the running of the office in the next few years. She worked so hard he had no doubt she would too.

He glanced at the couples swaying on the dance floor. 'I've enjoyed having Eliza and Tariq to stay too. Your sister seems very happy.'

Olivia followed his gaze and her smile softened as she watched Eliza and Tariq swaying in each other's arms. 'I miss her terribly now that she's living so far away. But she *is* happy and I'm so pleased for her. She, Tariq and little Ahmed make the perfect family for each other. I just knew she'd be a wonderful mother. And Ahmed is such a delicious baby!'

That made him grin. 'Brownie is in her element tonight looking after not just one, but two babies.'

He harboured no grudge for the deception the sisters had played on him. He'd forgiven Eliza the moment he'd held her tiny baby and she'd pronounced him Uncle Seb. 'We'll return the visit in a couple of months,' he promised.

He turned Olivia to face him more fully, both arms circling her waist. 'You haven't given me my birthday present yet.' She'd been working on it for weeks. 'Is it finished?'

A smile he couldn't read touched her lips. 'Oh, it's finished, but I thought you might prefer a private viewing rather than a public one.'

'Why?'

She took his hand and he followed silently as she led him through the house and up the stairs to their bedroom. A picture covered with a cloth hung on the wall opposite their four-poster bed.

He swallowed.

'Ready?'

He nodded.

The cloth fell away and he couldn't suppress a quick intake of breath. She'd painted him. Again. Nude.

He stared at it and his spine grew straighter, his shoulders broadened and his chin came up. 'You've made me look… You've made me look like the king of all I survey.'

She didn't say anything—just watched him as he continued to stare at the portrait.

It wasn't just that he looked supremely satisfied with his kingdom… 'You've made me look noble.'

'You are noble.'

While she'd painted him in a pose reminiscent of some mythical Greek god, the man in the portrait was unmistakably human—virile and alive. He looked like a king. He looked noble. And yet he pulsed with unmistakable sexual desire.

That same desire flooded every inch of Sebastian's being now—raw and scorching. He loved all the ways she saw him—all the ways she forced him to see himself. Not one of them was boring. She made him feel powerful and loved, and he wanted to give her everything.

He swung to her. A smile spread across her lips at whatever she saw in his eyes. 'You like it, then.'

'I love it,' he growled, advancing on her until she was backed up against one of the bedposts. He trailed lazy fingers down the deep neckline of her dress. The pulse in her throat fluttered to pounding life, and a primal triumph flooded him. 'I want to ravage you.'

She lifted her chin and her eyes glittered with desire. 'That's fortunate, because I'm in the mood to be ravaged.'

He claimed her lips and the passion between them flared to instant life—its intensity still had the potential to take him off guard.

When he lifted his head, long moments later, her eyes were as dark and needy as his must be.

She swallowed. 'I've been thinking…'

'I don't want you thinking,' he rasped. 'I want you mindless with sensation and pleasure.'

She huffed out a laugh, but her pupils dilated. 'You're a wicked man.'

He bit back a grin. 'Yes, but I'm your king.'

She tilted her chin. 'And I'm your queen.'

That was true. 'And what is it that my queen desires?' He pressed in closer, leaving her in no doubt what he desired.

He revelled in her quick intake of breath. His hands travelled the length of her back, his fingers digging into her hips to draw her closer. 'I just thought,' she panted, 'that it could be time to start adding to our family…to try for a baby.'

He stilled. He found it suddenly difficult to breathe. He craved a child with every atom he had, but… 'I don't want to rush you.'

She kinked an eyebrow. 'Maybe I want to rush you.'

No rushing necessary. Not on his part. He was almost too afraid to hope—he had so much already and… 'Are you sure?'

'I'm very sure.' She pulled his head down to hers, a smile in her eyes. 'Happy birthday, Seb.'

He kissed her with everything he had. He held her the way he meant to hold her for the rest of their lives. He loved her with a fire that would never go out.

'Are you sure,' she murmured against his mouth, 'that this isn't the best party you've ever had?'

Sebastian found himself laughing. 'What if I tell you it's one I'll never forget?'

Her eyes danced. 'That'll do, for now.' And then she pulled him down on the bed with her and it was a long time before either of them spoke again.

* * * * *

If you enjoyed this story, check out these other great reads from Michelle Douglas

SARAH AND THE SECRET SHEIKH
THE SPANISH TYCOON'S TAKEOVER
AN UNLIKELY BRIDE FOR
THE BILLIONAIRE
A DEAL TO MEND THEIR MARRIAGE

All available now!

Get 2 Free Books,
Plus 2 Free Gifts—
just for trying the Reader Service!